Praise for the Erskine Powell series

MALICE IN THE HIGHLANDS

"*Malice in the Highlands* is the perfect choice for readers nostalgic for the good old-fashioned British village mystery."

—*Alfred Hitchcock's Mystery Magazine*

MALICE IN CORNWALL

"The Cornish mists and sea swirl constantly in the background of *Malice in Cornwall*, a murder mystery that can also be read as a travel book. . . . Graham Thomas certainly knows how to exploit the air of romance, mystery, and danger that still hovers over Cornwall."

—SUSAN ALLEN TOTH
Author of *England for All Seasons*

MALICE ON THE MOORS

"Steeped in moor atmosphere, Thomas's novel is a traditional police procedural in the classic British sense."

—*The Snooper*

MALICE IN LONDON

"Jolly good reading for traditional British mystery buffs."

—*Meritorious Mysteries*

Also by Graham Thomas

MALICE IN THE HIGHLANDS
MALICE IN CORNWALL
MALICE ON THE MOORS
MALICE IN LONDON

MALICE
DOWNSTREAM

GRAHAM THOMAS

FAWCETT BOOKS • NEW YORK

A Fawcett Book
Published by The Ballantine Publishing Group
Copyright © 2002 by Gordon Kosakoski

www.ballantinebooks.com

ISBN 0-449-00709-X

Manufactured in the United States of America

First Edition: December 2002

10 9 8 7 6 5 4 3 2 1

With thanks to Christina Peressini
for the drawing of Houghton Bridge,
and to John Grindle of the Dorchester
Fishing Club for his hospitality.

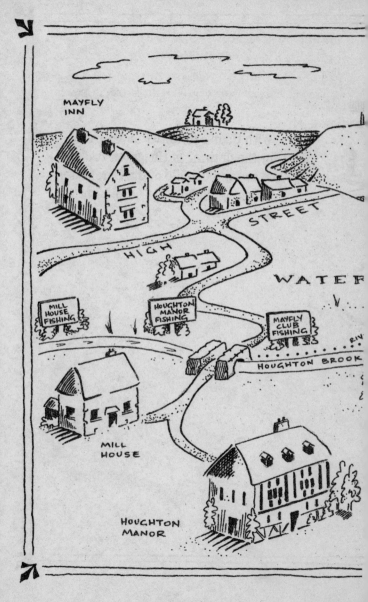

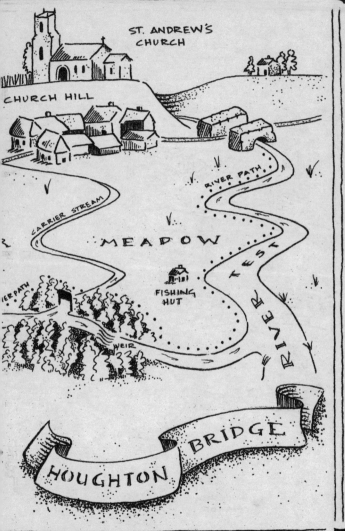

PROLOGUE

It was the sort of thing one could easily miss if one were unaccustomed to reading a river—the merest suggestion of a shadow flickering across a sliver of golden gravel in the center of the stream. A strand of weed possibly, momentarily displaced by some vagary of current, or perhaps nothing more than a ripple of refracted sunlight on the pebbled bottom. More likely than not it would simply have gone unnoticed—which was, of course, precisely the point.

For the shadow was caused by the sweep of a broad triangular tail belonging to a great trout that had made a successful career out of not being seen. For many years it had thrived in its short stretch of Hampshire chalk stream, growing long and fat and famous, no mean feat for a wild trout in these days of water abstraction, pollution, and Milquetoast hatchery fish.

The trout's cool curving world was bounded on the north by a copse of willow and hawthorn. On the south

1

side was a swath of open meadow edged with reeds, the source of the moving shadow-shapes he had learned to fear.

The upstream limit of the trout's demesne was marked by a stone bridge. On hot summer days he liked to rest in the pool beneath its cool arch where, safe from probing eyes, he would feed on drifting insects. The reach upstream of the bridge was largely *aqua incognita* into which he rarely ventured, lying as it did on the edge of his territorial horizon.

Below the Bridge Pool, the stream raced through a shallow run known as the Ford. Near the head of the run, a ramshackle fence, consisting of a few rusted strands of barbed wire strung on leaning wooden posts, straggled down the grassy bank and out into the middle of the stream before looping back to regain the top of the bank several yards farther downstream. The small enclosure thus formed was intended to confine watering cattle but it had served the trout well on more than one occasion.

Two hundred yards below the bridge, and effectively marking the downstream boundary of the trout's principality, was a low concrete weir. The trout would occasionally lie in the smooth cushion of water immediately upstream of the weir, rising sedately to suck in floating flies, but only during a prolific hatch when it was worth his while, and only then at dusk when he felt secure in the relatively shallow water.

On this particular day the trout was in the run below the Bridge Pool in about three feet of water just above the cattle fence. He had selected a favorite lie over a small patch of gravel between beds of swaying green *Ranunculus*. He held his position against the current without effort, his spotted back nearly invisible against the background of pebbles. His tail brushed occasionally against a submerged strand of barbed wire. Perhaps as a result of the warming effect of the spring sun on the water, the trout was alert, expectant. He sensed that something momentous was about to happen, something dimly associated in his primitive brain with both pleasure and pain. He was acutely aware of his surroundings: the pressure of the current against his sides, the rough scratch of gravel on his belly, the shimmering mirror of the water's surface, and directly above him the small blue window into another mysterious world.

The previous morning he had noticed an occasional large fly floating overhead—the succulent kind that appeared for only a short time each year. At first there were just a few of them in scattered flotillas of twos and threes, then they began to appear in increasing numbers until they covered the surface of the stream.

For a while, the trout had let them pass unmolested, unwilling to expend the energy to rise to the surface, content instead to root among the weeds for shrimp. Around midday, however, sensing perhaps that the hatch would soon be over, the trout rose sedately and sucked in one of the flies. As he turned back to his lie, crushing the insect against his tongue, he experienced the ecstasy of the first mayfly of the season. It was as if a switch had been thrown in his head. For the next two weeks he would feed on nothing but mayflies—the immature nymphs as they wriggled to the surface like tiny mermaids; the newly emerged duns, which floated on the water like miniature yellow sailboats until they were able to flutter away to safety; and the spent spinners that fell from the sky each evening to lay their eggs and die.

It was, in a perverse sort of way, this single-minded preoccupation with mayflies that led to the trout's demise a few days later. He had spent the morning gorging on duns, but just before noon he had an encounter with one of the shadow-shapes. He did not notice the glint of sunlight on the long rod until he turned after taking a particularly high-floating dun. But by then it was too late.

When he felt the sharp sting of the steel barb in the corner of his mouth he panicked, instinctively powering his way upstream against the pull of the line like a silver-flanked locomotive. Then spurred by some dim memory, he suddenly turned and, aided now by the current, ran downstream toward his tormentor. A moment later—whether by design or good fortune—he wrapped the line around a fence post and broke free.

For the remainder of the day the trout had sulked, lying motionless under the bridge. But with the onset of dusk he became emboldened and moved down to his usual spot just above the fence. The trout was still a bit skittish and not particularly interested in feeding. A few spinners floated past, glowing like tiny rubies in the dying light. But the great trout ignored them. The spinner fall grew heavier and soon the stream was covered with their twitching bodies and shining wings. And still the trout ignored them.

It all happened in a fateful instant—a tiny submerged creature drifting down upon him, too small for a mayfly nymph but vaguely suggesting something edible. If it *had* been a mayfly he would likely have let it pass, but because it was something unusual, something unexpected, he was caught off guard.

He snapped his jaws reflexively and took it, discovering instantly that it was not an insect at all but rather a size 14 hook wrapped with the fibers of a pheasant's tail and weighted with the kind of enameled copper wire used for winding electric motors. The hook pierced the trout's tongue and he burst from the water with a great commotion, scattering spray like shards of a broken mirror. He shook his head frantically in an attempt to free himself from the cruel kiss of this feathered Judas. He ran upstream just as he had that morning, but feeling no resistance this time, he stopped after a few yards, confused and alarmed. Turning downstream with the current he attempted to make a run for the fence, but was restrained by an inexplicable force that drew him inexorably upstream.

It was all over in a few minutes, his eyes turned inward as if in a final moment of self-awareness, then the chafe of the cotton net against his skin as he was lifted from the water, gills heaving, and delivered into the hands of his Charon.

CHAPTER 1

The village of Houghton Bridge straddled the River Test like a prim matron astride a winding serpent. At least that's the way Danica Hughes thought of it as she regarded the gray stone tower of the church, rising from the little hill above the High Street like an admonishing finger. She couldn't imagine what had possessed her to come home. Seven years was a long time, and seven years in London seemed like an eternity.

On the surface, Houghton Bridge remained the quintessential Hampshire village, or at least what passed for one nowadays. Set amidst idyllic surroundings, it boasted two traditional coaching inns, a family butcher, a bakery and teahouse, an antique shop, and even a Chinese restaurant for those adventurous souls whose tastes ran to the exotic. Houghton Bridge, like many other villages in the Test Valley, had once been the hub of a thriving agricultural community, supported by numerous family holdings employing a small army of farmworkers. But in the face of globalization—or whatever the current euphemism for greed unfettered by social responsibility was—these had all but disappeared, having been amalgamated into vast factory farms or given over to unattractive housing estates populated by townies who commuted daily to jobs in Andover and Winchester. Either way, the end result was the disappearance of a traditional way of life.

Earlier that afternoon she had walked to the end of the High Street and stood on the wide stone bridge that led to the Salisbury road. Silhouetted against a blustery gray sky, her long brown hair blowing wildly, she had gazed into the water for a long time, trying to reconcile the dingy stream flowing beneath her with the bright waters of her childhood. The Test of her memories was a lucent blue dream, more transparent than the sky itself, rushing over beds of shining chalk through lush water meadows spangled with wildflowers and butterflies. As a little girl she had imagined that the swaying waterweed was the long emerald hair of sprites and the huge trout that resided under every bridge were mischievous trolls.

She wondered how it had all gone so wrong. The river was now dark, depleted, and despoiled. The water meadows had been drained, and the flowers and butterflies had succumbed to pesticides. And not a day went by when she didn't think about Maggie and how it all might have ended differently.

When she returned to the cottage she was feeling more depressed than ever. As she sat watching the passersby from her window, she thought about Brian and how unfair it was to him. She looked at the clock and sighed. He would be home soon and she could use a drink. As she rose from her chair she noticed a movement at the corner of the window. It was a mayfly skittering along the sill. She placed her hand in its path and watched it climb onto her palm. She lifted her hand and examined it. It was a pale yellow dun about an inch long, its faintly colored wings exquisitely veined and delicate, set above a slender, arched abdomen with three long tails. Like Kate Moss with wings, she thought. *Ephemera danica,* the English mayfly, and her namesake. A beautiful name, she'd been told, but it seemed like a cruel joke now.

Being a riverkeeper's daughter she could see that it was a female—a virgin, in fact. It must have come from the small carrier that flowed beside the cottage. It had probably emerged from the cool depths of the stream earlier in the day and was destined to mate either that evening or the next. She thought about this lovely creature being set upon by a swarm of males and screwed senseless until it fluttered onto the water to lay its eggs. Then, with wings outstretched like a shining crucifix, she would die.

The girl gently closed her fingers around the dun. Its fluttering wings tickled her skin as it struggled to escape. She thought again about that day so long ago and the dark tunnel of the years that had led her back to Houghton Bridge.

She tightened her hand into a fist and squeezed as hard as she could, her eyes brimming with tears.

* * *

The scene appeared slightly out of focus, like a faded photograph—spidery black branches against a featureless sky and in the distance the buildings of the village huddled together beneath the stern tower of the church. She moved through the wet grass, stepping carefully over bloodred flowers. Her feet were bare and she was wearing a long white dress. The hem was soaked with dew and she noticed with a curious thrill of alarm that the damp stain had now risen above her knees. She shivered and began to hurry.

When eventually she stood beside the stream, rushing dark and deep between tangled banks, she called out in a small voice, "Maggie, Maggie!" There was no answer. There was never any answer, just a faceless figure in the distance, slowly approaching.

She stared at her dress, uncomprehending, as the dark stain crept past her waist. Her heart pounded, the metallic taste of fear in her throat. She closed her eyes. "Oh, God—Maggie," she whispered, "help me, please help me." She suddenly felt hot, feverish, her body warm and sticky now.

She opened her eyes and looked down. Her dress, drenched with blood, clung to her like a crimson shroud of self-immolation.

She knew that if she screamed she would not be able to stop.

"Dani, wake up. It's all right, I'm here." She felt the pressure of a hand on her shoulder, substantial and reassuring. Someone standing over her bed, a familiar voice.

"Maggie?" She struggled to get her bearings. Her shirt was soaked with perspiration, the duvet cast aside. The room was suffused with a gray light, a sliver of dawn between the curtains. Outside, the faint murmur of water.

"It's me, Brian," the voice persisted.

She remembered now. The Dream. The same dream she'd had every night since returning to Houghton Bridge.

"Are you all right?"

She sighed. "Yes, I'm fine."

He looked down at her, the halo of her dark hair and pale perfect skin, like Botticelli's Venus. He sat on the bed and reached for her hand. Her fingers were limp, unresponsive. "Dani, look . . . ," he said, "you can't go on like this."

"Can't I?" Her voice sounded oddly disinterested.

"You must stop blaming yourself," he persisted. "It's not your fault."

She searched his face. If only she could believe him.

"It happened a long time ago. Nothing either of us can do will bring her back—" He hesitated, groping for the right words. "I think you should talk to someone."

"Talk to someone?" Her voice was sharp now. "A bloody shrink? Is that what you mean?"

"Yes," he said quietly.

"And spend the rest of my days wandering about in a haze of antidepressants? No thank you." She experienced a sudden stab of guilt. "Oh, Brian, I—I'm so sorry. I didn't mean—"

He stopped her, shaking his head. "What's important right now is you."

She smiled weakly, trying to reassure him. "You've been very kind, letting me stay here until I can get settled. It's just that . . . there is nothing you or anybody else can do. I need to sort it out for myself."

He seemed strangely wounded by her words. "I understand, of course." There was an awkward silence. "Do you want me to stay?" he asked eventually.

She withdrew her hand from his. "I don't think that would be wise," she said, drawing the covers over her bare legs.

"No. No, I suppose not." He rose to his feet. "You'll let me know if you need anything?"

She attempted another smile. "I promise."

After he'd gone she stared at the ceiling for a long time, tears of recrimination burning her face.

CHAPTER 2

The old man sat on the bank of the Houghton Brook squinting into the sun. It was a glorious May morning; the meadow was alight with yellow cowslips and the pink sparks of ragged robin; warblers chattered in the reeds, and the stream was running full and clear. The first flowering tresses of *Ranunculus* had emerged onto the surface of the water, turning the weed beds white with delicate flowers. The man looked at his companion. "What do you think, John, was it a dabchick or a fish?"

John Miller, head riverkeeper for the Mayfly Fishing Club, studied the concentric ripples spreading over the surface of the water. "I'm certain it's a fish, Sir Robert."

Sir Robert nodded. "Right. There are a few olives coming off. Shall I stick with the Adams?"

"Should be as good as anything. Try to place your fly even with that patch of reeds, no more than a foot out from the bank, if you can. You'll have to watch you don't get caught up." Miller considered the position. It was a

12

difficult cast for a right-handed caster, casting upstream from the left bank of the stream, but he was confident that Sir Robert could pull it off. Of all the members of the club, he most enjoyed guiding Sir Robert. The old boy was getting on now, but he was an accomplished angler who had spent fifty years perfecting his technique on the best trout stream in the world and—more important of all as far as Miller was concerned—he possessed a deep and abiding love for the sport.

The Mayfly Club, established in 1821, was arguably the most exclusive fishing club in the world. Membership was limited to nineteen, and it counted among its members peers of the realm, captains of industry, doctors, lawyers, military men, and politicians past and present— the top drawer of British society, in Miller's estimation. Only three things were needed for one to be considered for membership in the Mayfly Club: money, connections, and—since members were elected for life—someone had to die first.

The Mayfly Club owned exclusive fishing rights on twelve miles of the River Test and rented the rights on its tributary, the Houghton Brook. The club also owned a modern trout hatchery for stocking the river, and several local businesses including the Mayfly Inn in Houghton Bridge, which served as the club's headquarters during the fishing season. The club's affairs were managed by an honorary secretary, usually the longest-standing member, while the business of maintaining the fishery was overseen by the head riverkeeper, who supervised a number of assistant keepers.

As Miller watched his gentleman work out a suitable length of line with crisp false-casts, he realized just how lucky he was. He was able to make a living at a job he loved and, the son of a farmworker, he had achieved a station in life he had never dreamed possible. *J. R. Miller, Riverkeeper, Testbourne House, Houghton Bridge, Hants.* At first he'd had a problem with the upstairs-downstairs aspect of the job, but the social climate was changing in Britain, and class was less of an issue nowadays. Admittedly, the members tended to be fairly conservative and some of them liked to lord it over mere mortals like himself, but generally the relationship between the riverkeeper and his employers was a cordial one based on mutual respect.

To Miller, Sir Robert Alderson epitomized the classic Mayfly Club member. The eldest son of an old East Sussex family, Sir Robert was a distinguished surgeon, now retired, who had been knighted for making some breakthrough or other in the field of organ transplantation. Above all he was a true gent. Soft-spoken and equable by nature, and progressive in his ideas, Sir Robert always gave the impression that whomever he was speaking to was, at that particular moment, the most important person in the world. He was presently the club's honorary secretary and, as such, worked closely with the riverkeeper on the management of the fishery. He had supported Miller's recommendation, against considerable opposition from some of the other members, to reduce the stocking of hatchery fish in order to increase the head of wild trout in the club's water. This had forged a bond

between them, which had led on several occasions to Sir
Robert seeking Miller's advice on internal club affairs,
confidential matters that the riverkeeper would never have
dreamed of discussing with anyone else, not even his
wife. Another point in Sir Robert's favor was the fact that
he was by far the best dry fly fisherman in the Mayfly
Club, almost as good as himself, Miller reckoned, not im-
modestly.

"Here we go," Sir Robert said with a final forward snap
of his rod.

It was a beautiful cast; the line and leader straightened
in the air before dropping the tiny fly like a wisp of down
on the water about a yard upstream of where the fish had
last risen. Sir Robert drew in line at exactly the same pace
as the fly drifted back toward him. One moment the fly
was floating on the surface of the stream, wings cocked
upright, and the next moment it had disappeared, leaving
only a sprinkling of tiny bubbles behind.

"God Save the Queen," Sir Robert intoned in a mea-
sured cadence to give the fish time to take the fly firmly.
Then he raised his rod sharply to set the hook.

Stung by the barb, the trout tore downstream toward
the weir at the bottom end of the beat. The rod bowed and
the reel screeched as the fish stripped off line.

"You'd better turn him, Sir Robert," Miller said matter-
of-factly. "Another ten yards and he'll be over."

Sir Robert nodded. "Right."

He gradually applied pressure with his forefinger to the
drum of the reel to slow its revolution and then, holding
his breath, he clamped down hard. The little split cane rod

bent double but miraculously nothing broke. After having been so abruptly pulled up short, the fish seemed content to stay where it was and sulk. Sir Robert slowly got to his feet and made his way downstream, stooping slightly and keeping just the right amount of pressure on the fish— enough to keep it off-balance but not enough to provoke it into running again. When he was directly opposite, he coaxed it to the bank without further incident.

Miller scooped the trout up in the net and presented it to his gentleman. "A cracking fish, Sir Robert. A little over two pounds, I should think. That makes a brace for the morning." He paused, awaiting instructions.

The fisherman examined his catch appreciatively. It was indeed a splendid specimen, about sixteen inches long and deep in the body, with gold on its belly, irides- cent purple flanks sprinkled with dark spots, and a broad green back. "Let's release it," he said. "One will be enough for supper."

"Right." The riverkeeper knelt beside the stream and gently returned the trout to the water. He watched it slowly swim away, none the worse for the wear and tear but perhaps a little wiser. He looked up at Sir Robert. "Shall I put the kettle on?"

Sir Robert smiled. "Splendid."

As they sat together on the bench outside the rustic fishing hut, Sir Robert turned to the riverkeeper. "You're a lucky man, John," he said with conviction.

Miller thought about this for a moment, a seemingly odd statement coming from a man in Sir Robert's position. But he knew that his companion wasn't referring to money or power or influence. He let his gaze wander from the sparkling stream, across the lush sweep of meadow and up to the high green downs dotted with constellations of white sheep. The riverkeeper nodded. "I won't argue with you, Sir Robert. To get paid for doing something you'd do for nothing is a privilege." He grinned. "But don't tell any of the other members I said that."

Sir Robert laughed. "Your secret is safe with me." He drained his mug and made a contented sound. "There is absolutely nothing like a cuppa at a time like this." Then he cleared his throat, his expression turned suddenly serious. "John, I'd like your advice on something, a little matter of club business. Strictly on the q.t., you understand."

"Of course, Sir Robert."

"You are aware that there is presently a vacancy in our ranks. . . ."

The riverkeeper nodded. Mr. Brian St. John-MacDonald, Q.C. had passed away last year—a heart attack, he'd been told—and his replacement had yet to be announced.

Sir Robert lowered his voice in a conspiratorial manner. "There are three candidates being considered. You remember Stephen Solomon? He's fished as Reynolds's guest on several occasions."

Miller nodded.

"Only one stain on his escutcheon, as far as I can tell . . . ," Sir Robert said in a neutral voice. He paused, regarding the riverkeeper speculatively. "Another bloody stockbroker."

"I guided him and Mr. Reynolds last season," Miller volunteered. "We had an excellent day."

Sir Robert looked relieved. "The second candidate is a former student of mine—runs a leading biotech firm now. Developed a new type of heart valve, don't you know. My nominee, in fact." He paused. "Her name's Jemma Walker."

Miller raised an eyebrow. "Jemma?"

"Wonderful girl! Been like a granddaughter to me. And a first-class fly fisherman to boot," he added with boyish enthusiasm.

The riverkeeper hardly knew what to say. A woman? In the Mayfly Club?

"Nothing like change to shake things up a little, I always say," Sir Robert pronounced.

Shake things up? More like a ten on the Richter scale, Miller thought.

Sir Robert was smiling. "Don't look so shocked, John."

"Don't get me wrong, Sir Robert, but do you really think she—Ms. Walker, I mean—has a chance?"

Sir Robert sighed. "Not this time around, I'm afraid. But one must fight the good fight nonetheless. I'm not one for political correctness and all that rubbish, but I do believe we need to break the mold and open ourselves up to new ideas and different viewpoints. Like any institution, the Mayfly Club must change with the times if it's to survive."

"I couldn't agree more, Sir Robert—" The riverkeeper was distracted by a mayfly fluttering overhead. He glanced at his watch. Time to shift before the hatch started in earnest. "Er, you mentioned that there were three candidates, Sir Robert," he prompted.

His companion frowned slightly. "Oh, yes. The third candidate is Richard Garrett." He hesitated. "Nominated by his father, of course."

The riverkeeper stared at him, his mind awhirl with conflicting emotions. The memories he had tried to suppress for so many years suddenly welled up, threatening to overwhelm him. He got slowly to his feet and handed Sir Robert his rod. "We should be going, Sir Robert," he said in a flat voice. "We don't want to miss the rise."

CHAPTER 3

"I'm not sure I understand, sir," Detective-Sergeant Bill Black said slowly, setting his glass carefully on the patio table. "I mean, why is it that you can only fish in an upstream direction? Is it considered more sporting?"

"Yes and no," Chief Superintendent Erskine Powell replied vaguely, wondering how one could possibly discuss the arcane conventions of dry fly fishing with someone who was not already an acolyte. He looked out over the untidy expanse of his back garden. Black's wife, Mildred, was bustling round the vegetable patch seeking out the few scraggly spring onions that had not been choked to death by weeds. She clucked disapprovingly to herself. "Can I give you a hand?" Powell sang out cheerily.

She looked up at him, the corners of her mouth turning up in spite of herself. "You'd better keep off that leg, Mr. Powell. As soon as I'm done, I'll start dinner."

Powell looked at Black and spoke in his best Middle English, *"What is bettre than wisdom? Womman. And what is better than a good womman? No-thing."*

Black grinned, rising to the occasion. *"Disguise our bondage as we will, 'Tis woman, woman, rules us still."* His evening classes in English Literature Appreciation coupled with a near-photographic memory rarely let him down in these literary sparring matches with his superior.

"Bravo!" Powell exclaimed. "This calls for another drink."

Black reached for their glasses. "Here, let me do it, sir."

It occurred to Powell as he lit another cigarette that life—even a solitary one in Surbiton—wasn't so bad. True, his wife, Marion, was away in Canada on sabbatical until the end of the summer, but she had been home to see him last month, even if the circumstances hadn't been exactly ideal with him flat on his back in hospital nursing a septic leg the size of an elephant's. He absently rubbed his right thigh; still a bit tender but definitely on the mend. Looking on the bright side, it could have been much worse and, when all was said and done, temporary invalidism did have its advantages. Like having the Blacks come round to fix him dinner.

His reverie was interrupted by the return of Detective-Sergeant Black. The stocky policeman set the drinks on the table—a whisky for Powell and a lager for himself—and eased himself back into his chair. He raised his glass. "Well, cheers, Mr. Powell. Here's to Hampshire."

"Cheers." Powell took an appreciative sip. "It'll be a

pleasant interlude before returning to the salt mines." Not half, he thought. A week ensconced in a charming B&B in a picturesque Hampshire village on the banks of the River Test. Not to mention the fact that he had been invited to partake in a few days' fishing as the guest of an old university chum—during mayfly season, at that. It all seemed too good to be true, which in Powell's experience was a fairly reliable indication that it probably was. In fact, when he examined the prospect more closely, there was a tiny dark cloud on the horizon. He looked at Black, his expression turning suddenly grim. "You know, Bill," he said, "I keep expecting Merriman to ring at any moment to tell me he's torn up my sick-note."

Powell was convinced that his superior, Sir Henry Merriman, assistant commissioner of the Metropolitan Police Service, had it in for him—a conviction that remained undiminished by the knowledge that Merriman treated everyone in his charge equally badly.

Black watched Powell closely. Time to change the subject, he thought, having grown accustomed over the years to his superior's mercurial moods. "Sir?" he inquired brightly.

Powell sighed heavily. "Yes, Black, what is it?"

"The upstream dry fly—I still don't get it."

"Oh, that. The glorious legacy of Mr. Halford." Powell went on to explain how at the beginning of the last century a fierce battle had raged between the two leading anglers of the day, Frederick Halford and G. E. M. Skues, concerning the most effective method for catching trout in English chalk streams. Halford, who fished the River Test, perfected the technique of casting upstream with a floating fly intended to mimic exactly whatever insect the trout was feeding on at the time. Skues, on the other hand, fishing his beloved Itchen, advocated the use of a more impressionistic fly called a nymph, cast upstream as well but sunk beneath the surface. Halford's dogma eventually prevailed, but things became so heated that Skues was banned on some rivers. "In these permissive times of ours," Powell concluded dryly, "both methods are considered acceptable."

Black shook his head, looking slightly perplexed. "But, sir, it's only *fishing.*"

Powell took another sip of Scotch. "And this," he rejoined, "is only drinking."

Black persisted. "You still haven't explained why you can't fish a fly *downstream.*"

"It's just not done, old man. If you were caught indulging in such a depraved act, you'd be thrashed to within an inch of your life with your own fly rod."

Black chuckled. "I think I'll stick to coarse fishing."

Powell drew deeply on his cigarette. "There *is* a good reason for the upstream rule, of course. Chalk streams like the Test are renowned for their exceptional clarity. As a consequence, the trout that live in them—at least those with the wit to survive more than a season or two—are pretty skittish. Once frightened, they can become uncatchable for hours. Since a trout lying in a stream always faces into the current, an angler situated on the bank behind the fish cannot be seen and can therefore cast upstream with relative impunity. An angler fishing downstream, on the other hand, runs the risk of being spotted, ruining his own sport as well as the chances of anyone coming after him. There *are* occasions when a downstream cast is the only way to cover a fish—a fish lying in a culvert, for instance—but as a general rule, it's a dubious practice, presenting considerable risk with little chance of success."

"Much like police work, then," Detective-Sergeant Black remarked.

Powell regarded his able but somewhat stodgy assistant with a look of mild amusement. "Yes, Black, much like police work."

Monday afternoon, the day before he was to leave for Hampshire, Powell took the train into Waterloo Station. He stared out the window for the entire journey, preoccupied with his thoughts. Twenty minutes later he was in Charlotte Street, drawn there, he suspected in a moment of whimsy, by a subliminal electronic siren call emanating from the looming British Telecom Tower. He found himself powerless to resist as he was swept through the doorway of the Fitzrovia Tavern and dashed helplessly against the oak-paneled bar. There were a few regulars seated at tables and a young couple cooing at each other next to him at the bar.

Celia Cross, the blowsy proprietor, beamed when she saw him. "That leg's looking much better, Mr. Powell."

He leaned his walking stick against the bar. "Thank you for noticing, Celia. Most people put my condition down to advancing age and general decrepitude. A pint of the usual, I think."

"Coming right up." She completed the task with the utmost concentration, then placed the glass in front of him. "This one's on the 'ouse, Mr. Powell. For old times' sake."

His previous case had involved a former barmaid at the Fitzrovia Tavern and had very nearly cost him his leg, not to mention his bloody neck. "Very kind of you, Celia. You are—" He was interrupted by the departure of the young couple, who groped each other enthusiastically as they hurried out the door.

"Ah, to be young again," Powell observed, raising his glass to take a lengthy sip.

Celia shook her head. "I wouldn't turn back the clock for all the tea in China. There's much to be said for the wisdom of maturity, Mr. Powell. Reason over passion, I always say."

"Really?" Powell rejoined. "I must ask Mr. Cross about that."

She gave him a disapproving look. "You know what I mean. It's like them two that just went out. When you're snogging in a car with the windows all fogged up, you can't see a thing outside. But when you get older, it's like you've wiped the windows clean and you can see for the first time what's really important in life."

Powell smiled. "You haven't been ordained since I last saw you, have you?"

She frowned. "Mark my words, Mr. Powell, I see it every day in this job. People who don't know 'ow lucky they are, sitting 'ere drowning their sorrows."

He raised an eyebrow. "Are you trying to tell me something, Celia?"

She shrugged. "It's all part of the service."

"Another pint, I think, to sustain me whilst I count my blessings."

She looked skeptical. "Right."

CHAPTER 4

It was some time later that Powell made his way unsteadily across Windmill Street to the K2 Tandoori.

He was welcomed warmly at the door by a slight, dark man with a neatly trimmed mustache and a military bearing. "Erskine, my dear chap, this is indeed a surprise. It is fortunate that you came early, for we are nearly booked up tonight."

"Sorry, Rashid, I really should have called ahead. I hope it's not a problem. . . ."

"Of course not, my friend. Here, let me take your jacket." The restaurateur regarded Powell with fond concern. A few pints in him, by the look of it, and needing a curry to warm his heart before returning to his lonely house.

A few moments later Powell was settled at his usual table near the window, sipping a Cobra lager and munching on a *poppadum* amidst the aromatic ambience of polished brass, potted palms, and recorded sitar music. On the wall above his table was an exotic print depicting a turbaned maharaja doing something acrobatically but tastefully erotic with his bejeweled maharani. Glancing around, he estimated that the restaurant was three-quarters full even though it was still early. Although off the beaten tourist track north of Soho, the K2 Tandoori enjoyed a growing reputation as *the* place to go for Indian food in central London, with an eccentric and flamboyant host thrown in at no extra cost. Powell viewed the popularity of his favorite restaurant with mixed feelings. He had been coming to the K2 for over twenty years, long before the red flock wallpaper had given way to silk, and tended to regard it as his private club, a snug harbor protected from the squalls of everyday life. He supposed in a way that he resented the fact that he had to book ahead these days, although he certainly didn't begrudge Rashid his well-earned success.

His host soon joined him, and they chatted about this and that. But it wasn't long before Rashid concluded that Powell had something on his mind. He had learned over the years that his old friend was a very private person— to a fault, one might even say—but despite his English reserve, Powell always gave the impression that he valued Rashid's advice, which the restaurateur was never reluctant to offer.

"You are looking considerably more spry since I last saw you, my friend," Rashid pronounced.

"Soon be right as rain. I should be back at work in a couple of weeks."

"I imagine you are thrilled to death with the prospect."

"Wild horses couldn't hold me back."

Rashid grinned. "And how are Marion and the boys?"

"Marion called last night. She hopes to finish up her research by the end of July. She wants me to go out there in August for a family holiday."

Rashid sighed. "That sounds wonderful indeed. I have a cousin who lives in British Columbia. He is a lumberjack, I think."

Powell resisted the temptation to launch into a rendition of the Monty Python song. "Yes, well, I understand they do have a lot of trees," he said.

"Will you go?"

Powell shrugged. "Why not? It's a chance to see a bit more of the world, and I haven't seen Peter and David since they were all home at Christmas."

Rashid got the distinct impression that Powell was not exactly thrilled with the prospect of a trip to Canada. He motioned to one of his waiters for another Cobra. He bit his tongue and waited for Powell to speak.

Powell lit a cigarette and studied his friend's earnest expression. He smiled. "Sometimes I think you know me better than I know myself, Rashid." He drew deeply on his cigarette. "Marion's been offered an assistant professorship at the University of British Columbia."

Rashid's eyes widened. He seemed uncharacteristically at a loss for words. Eventually he stammered, "W-would she—I mean could she—would you . . ." He trailed off awkwardly.

"I think she is seriously considering the offer," Powell said neutrally. "It's a tremendous opportunity for her.

West Coast native culture is her specialization, and where better than British Columbia to pursue her studies? It's pretty clear that the boys want to stay in Canada after they finish university, and I get the impression that Marion has become enamored with the place as well. In any case, she has asked me to think about it."

"Would you actually go?" Rashid asked, his voice hushed. "I mean, what would you do there?"

Powell shrugged. "Perhaps I could open an Indian restaurant in Vancouver." He paused. "Or maybe get a job as a security guard."

Rashid could not decide whether or not his friend was being flippant. He frowned. "But shouldn't a wife—?" he checked himself.

Powell said nothing because there was nothing to say. At least nothing he could say to Rashid—or to anyone else, for that matter—about the increasingly barren years after his sons had grown and gone. When he and Marion had shared a house but not their lives.

"But how could you ever leave England?" Rashid asked, obviously deeply troubled.

Powell sighed. "Aye, there's the rub—"

They were interrupted by the appearance of a young waiter bearing a beer for the distinguished-looking customer and an orange squash for his overbearing boss. "Thank you, please," he said as he replenished Powell's glass under Rashid's stern gaze.

Rashid realized that this was not the time to wallow in it—his friend clearly had more than enough on his mind—but a time rather for celebrating what was great

about this damn bloody country despite the deplorable
state of British cricket, the general decline in decorum,
and the traitorous abdication of power to the paper wal-
lahs in Brussels. He looked at Powell and grinned. "Fish
and chip shops," he pronounced.

"What?"

"Brown sauce!" he prompted.

Powell smiled in spite of himself. "Marmite," he ventured.

"Green wellies."

"Barbour jackets."

"*Les Mis.*"

Powell grimaced. "Yes, well, test matches," he rejoined.

Rashid shook his head sadly. "That is hitting below the
belt, my friend. Now let me see . . . cream teas!"

"Chicken tika *masala.*"

"Her majesty."

"Liz Hurley."

"Mohammed Al Fayed."

"Lord Archer."

"Bangers and mash."

"Spotted dick—by the way, I hope this isn't some sort
of psychological word association test," Powell remarked.

"Lager louts," Rashid continued gleefully.

"Best bitter."

"Football hooligans."

" 'The Campaign for Real Ale.' "

"British Rail."

Powell laughed. "God help us if it comes down to that."

"Rashid's dark eyes sparkled. "You see, my friend, at least we can still laugh."

"No so fast, Rashid, it's still my turn." He paused for effect. "The K2 Tandoori in Charlotte Steet, W1, London."

Rashid's eyes glistened. "You are very kind, my friend."

"Now, then," Powell continued briskly, "I am absolutely famished and I don't wish to keep you from your other patrons." He glanced at the menu as he always did, although he knew it from memory. "Let me see . . . vegetable *samosas* to start, I think, followed by *achari gosht,* rice *pilau,* and a *naan.*"

Rashid nodded graciously. "I will go now and personally prepare your dinner," he said, getting to his feet. "More *poppadums* for Mr. Powell!" he barked to no one in particular as he disappeared through the swinging doors at the rear of the restaurant, providing a glimpse into the clattering chaos of the kitchen, which looked for all the world like the engine room of some hellish steamship.

Powell found it difficult to concentrate on his newspaper as he waited for his meal. He attempted, with a similar lack of success, to confine his attention to the week ahead. His thoughts kept returning to his marriage and his two sons. Marion and he had gradually grown apart over the years, the space between them widening as the boys got older. Increasingly they had immersed themselves in their careers to fill the vacuum in their marriage. Looking back on it now, he could see it all so clearly. On the positive side of the ledger, Peter and David had turned out to be fine young men, both of them more emotionally balanced than their father—more like their mother, to give Marion her due—and that was all that really mattered. Despite their problems, he had supposed that at the end of it all he and Marion would drift into comfortable senility together on separate but parallel tracks to the grave.

He had been caught completely off guard by the choice that now confronted him, and he wondered in God's name what he was going to do.

CHAPTER 5

John Miller stood in the tiny fishing hut on the bank of the River Test brewing a cup of tea. The sibilant whistle of the kettle was punctuated periodically by the squawk of a cock pheasant in the field across the river. It was early, nearly two hours before the first fisherman would turn up at the beat. There was a damp chill in the air, and the meadow was covered with a thick blanket of mist. He glanced out the window at the gray, featureless sky and reckoned that the fog should burn off by midmorning. He frowned, unable to dispel the nagging feeling that he had forgotten to do something important.

Normally, May was the riverkeeper's favorite time of year, the culmination of all the hard work that had gone before. The so-called "closed" season from the beginning of October to the end of March was in fact his busiest time. October, when the water was at its lowest and clearest, was the time for electric fishing to remove the pike, those voracious and most unwelcome predators of trout. This was followed by the autumn weed cut to trim back the growth that had occurred since the last cut in August. Weeds were a mixed blessing from a riverkeeper's point of view; they provided habitat for the aquatic insects that fed the trout, but too much growth could literally choke the life out of the river. Another important job during this period was collecting trout for brood stock, stripping and incubating the eggs, and then tending the young fish in the hatchery stew ponds. A final weed cut in the early spring followed by the release of the hatchery fry and he could begin to relax and focus on the fishing, which of course was the whole point of the exercise. Miller took immense pride in this work and always looked forward to the climax of the fishing in May—the Mayfly Carnival, as he called it. But on that particular morning as he waited in the fishing hut, he felt on edge, the same feeling he got just before an electric storm was about to break.

He had set out early hoping to see her. He knew that she usually went for a walk along the river path before breakfast and he wanted it to look like a chance encounter, not something planned or calculated. He felt a bit foolish—he could simply have paid her a visit at Brian's, but that might have been a bit awkward under the circumstances. Ever since she had returned to Houghton Bridge he had wanted to find some excuse to see her, to find out why she had come back, while at the same time dreading her answer. The more he thought about her, the more he had begun to question his own motives. Wasn't it better to leave sleeping dogs lie? He had built a good life for himself in Houghton Bridge and had a wife and two small children to think about—

His thoughts were interrupted by the thud of boots outside the hut. He turned slowly toward the doorway.

"Hello, John."

He swallowed. She was as breathtakingly lovely as he remembered her. "Hello, Danica."

She smiled. "A cup of tea would be nice."

"Yes, of course."

She sat down on the bench against the wall opposite the window. Along the wall under the window was a counter with a small primus cooker on it, a blackened kettle, several mugs and assorted spoons, a bowl of sugar, and a tin of milk. The riverkeeper set about making the tea. He turned to her. "Milk, but no sugar, right?"

"You remember."

He searched her face for hidden meaning as he handed her a mug.

"Ta." She held the steaming cup in both hands and took a grateful swallow.

"How was London?"

"Bloody awful."

"I can imagine."

"Can you? For the past seven years my life has been populated with fuckwits, perverts, and alcoholics."

"Danica, I—"

"I was up to see Father the other day," she interrupted. "He asked about you during one of his more lucid moments. Half the time I don't think he even knew who I was."

"I must try and get up to see him," Miller said awkwardly.

"He'd like that. He always thought we'd end up together, you know."

Miller didn't know what to say.

She fixed him with those striking blue eyes, as clear and shining as the Houghton Brook itself. "How have you been keeping, John?"

"Can't complain."

"I hear you're married now." Her voice matter-of-fact.

He swallowed. "Yes, a girl named Laura Smith. I don't think you know her—she used to teach school in Stockbridge. We have two little ones: a boy, two, and a girl, four."

She considered this for a moment. "Are you happy?" she asked, her eyes never leaving his.

"Yes, very," he replied without hesitating.

She brushed a strand of hair from her face. "I'm glad, John, I really am. In fact, I envy you. You've been able to put everything behind you. I wish I could."

He felt a twinge of worry. "You're wrong, Danica, I've just learned to accept things."

Her expression hardened. "Well, I can't do that. I think about it every day and I'll never accept it."

"How do you think I feel?" he asked, his face burning. "The fact is, nothing either one of us can do will bring her back. End of story."

She stood up abruptly. "It's been nice talking to you, John. I really should be going."

He cleared his throat. "Yes, well, we'll have to get together sometime. . . ." He felt like an idiot.

After she had gone, he stood rigidly outside the hut staring into the mist.

Simon Street leaned his back against the mantelpiece and lit his pipe. Fortyish, with striking aquiline features, he looked younger than his years. He was wearing a tweed jacket, immaculately pressed moleskin trousers, and a pair of brogues that were just scuffed enough not to look new.

"Why don't you sit down," his wife said irritably. "You look like an advert for gracious living."

"I am, actually," he said between puffs, regarding her with a languid air. "I must say, Pamela, you seem a bit pensive this evening."

"You'll never guess who I saw in the High Street today," she said vaguely.

He stifled a yawn. "Pray tell, my little cabbage."

"Robert Alderson."

This seemed to catch Street's attention. "Oh, yes?"

"He told me that Richard Garrett is coming down for the fishing this year."

Street's expression darkened. "That little bastard better not show his face around here."

"Apparently he's been nominated for membership in the club."

Street looked at her with a brittle smile. "I hadn't heard. You obviously move in more rarefied circles than I do."

"You are such a snob, Simon."

"That is what makes this country great, my dear. Everyone in their place."

She sighed wearily. She didn't have the energy to pursue the point. Besides, she couldn't remember why she had raised the subject in the first place. She crossed her legs and smoothed her skirt with her hand. "Get me a sherry, would you."

He smiled. "Coming right up, my sweet. You look like you could use a very large one."

He set his pipe down on the mantel, then strode over to the drinks cupboard. He returned a few moments later with her glass.

"Won't you join me?" she asked.

"I think not. Must keep the faculties sharp. Did I tell you that Alan has sent me a script? It's by an up-and-coming young playwright . . . can't remember his name now, but he's very much in demand apparently. I've had a quick look at it. A bit Pinteresque, perhaps—you know, monosyllabic dialogue with pregnant pauses you could drive a train through—but much better than the usual shit I'm asked to consider. I'll give it a good read this evening, and if it measures up . . . well, you never know, my precious"—he gestured grandly—"the triumphant return of Simon Street to the West End may soon be in the offing."

She downed her sherry with a single gulp. "That's nice, dear." She sounded bored.

He stood over her. "You are such a bitch, Pamela," he observed in a matter-of-fact voice. "You don't believe me, do you?"

"I—I just don't want you to get your hopes up, dear."

"You do realize, Pamela, that we could use the extra money."

A sudden look of alarm in her eyes.

Street smiled reassuringly. "Don't worry, my sweet. Things will work out in the end." He bent over and kissed her neck, resting his hand on her thigh. He slid it higher. "You're so tense," he murmured, "and we still have an hour or so before dinner."

CHAPTER 6

The train trip from London to Winchester was un-
eventful if one discounts the excitement generated by
thirty or so energetic schoolchildren on an outing to see
the cathedral, running from car to car, spilling their
drinks on the other passengers. When Powell stepped
onto the platform at Winchester Station, juggling his bag
and fishing rod amidst a stampede of little uniformed
storm troopers, a familiar figure approached him, grin-
ning broadly.

The man extended his hand. He was about Powell's
age, donnish-looking with tousled gray hair and a tweed
jacket. "Long time no see, Erskine."

Powell smiled. "Hello, Jim."

The man relieved Powell of his bag. "My car is just
outside," he said. They exchanged pleasantries as they
made their way to the station exit.

A few moments later they piled into his estate wagon and
were soon speeding along the A272 through undulating

green countryside. Powell had roomed with Jim Hardy at Cambridge, and although they hadn't had a lot in common they had gotten along together well enough. Apart from bumping into each other at a reunion of their college several years back, however, they hadn't kept in touch. Hardy had apparently learned about Powell's injury from a mutual friend in London and had decided to ring his old roommate and invite him down to Hampshire for a few days' fishing. "Just what the doctor ordered," he had promised. "I've got a spare guest room and you're welcome to it for as long as you want."

Powell had accepted with alacrity, but had to admit to being a bit curious about how Hardy had ended up running a B&B.

Hardy smiled. "That, as they say, is a long story. I'll give you the *Reader's Digest* version. I was teaching at a small public school up north and not enjoying it very much—it didn't take me long to realize that a working knowledge of Latin was fairly low on the priority list of my young charges. Anyway, I decided to chuck it all in. It was a bit impulsive, really. I hadn't a clue what I wanted to do with the rest of my life—you know, the usual midlife crisis—my marriage was on the rocks, and I was feeling pretty desperate. However, as often happens in such situations, a convenient life raft came floating by. A kindly aunt of mine passed on, leaving me a modest inheritance. And as chance would have it, one of my colleagues at the school had mentioned that his brother-in-law had a small guesthouse in Hampshire up for sale. To make a long story short, I decided to take the plunge.

That was almost ten years ago now and I've never looked back. It's funny how things turn out. Fancy me running a tourist trap and you a copper, both of us with degrees in classics. It's enough to restore one's faith in the British educational system."

"Nam et ipsa scientia potestas est," Powell observed.

Hardy laughed. *"Rem acu tetigisti!"*

Powell thought it best to quit while he was ahead. He inquired about the fishing.

"The mayflies have just started, so your timing is perfect."

"I'm a bit rusty when it comes to dry fly fishing," Powell admitted.

His companion grinned. "Not to worry. It's 'duffer's fortnight,' as we like to refer to it in these parts. If you can't catch a trout when the mayflies are hatching, you never will."

"That *is* comforting," Powell rejoined drily.

Hardy looked embarrassed. "I didn't mean to suggest that you weren't—" He suddenly shifted down with a clashing of gears as the road began its plunge from the high downs to the valley below. The rolling green and yellow checkerboard of grain fields and oil-seed rape soon gave way to gushing streams and lush meadows as they descended the steep scarp.

"The downs are basically a great mass of porous chalk, sort of like a giant sponge," Hardy explained as he negotiated the winding road. "The rain falls up on top, filters through eventually and pops out down here as springs. The springs feed the rivulets that feed the streams and so on. The water is gin-clear, loaded with minerals, and has a constant temperature of fifty-one degrees. Perfect for growing trout."

Powell noticed that his companion had a rather alarming habit of watching him instead of the road as he chatted away. Gripping his seat, Powell kept his eyes fixed straight ahead, making interested noises at the appropriate times.

"And did you know," Hardy continued in schoolmasterish fashion, "that the Test itself is for the most part an artificial canal dug through the old water meadows by the Romans—" He braked suddenly as a lovely old inn of whitewashed brick with blue-trimmed bow windows came into view, then he swerved into a narrow tree-lined lane. "Houghton Bridge," he announced. "That was the Mayfly Inn. If you follow the main road you'll come to the High Street and the Test Bridge. My place is just up here a tick."

The road skirted a lush meadow on their left and a little farther on they crossed a bright little stream with crystal currents and absinthe green weeds.

"The Houghton Brook?" Powell asked.

"Three miles of paradise, or in our case a little less than three hundred yards. Better fishing than the Test, in my opinion. But you'll see for yourself soon enough."

Powell could not suppress his curiosity. "If you don't mind me asking, how did you manage to acquire the fishing?"

Hardy looked at him with an amused expression. "How could I afford it, you mean?"

Powell smiled. "Yes, if you like."

"Well, I should dispel any notion that I am independently wealthy—one would probably be looking at something in excess of a million pounds for fishing of this quality. To answer your question, the fishing comes with the guesthouse. Courtesy of the lady of the manor, Pamela Street. We just passed her place, the big house up there on the left."

Powell looked back and caught a glimpse of sprawling Tudor gables and chimneys.

"It was a tradition begun by her late husband, Colonel Waddington," Hardy continued. "As long as Mill House was operated as a hostelry, the colonel was happy to provide fishing for the guests. The old boy died a few years before I bought the place but, happily, Mrs. Street has continued the tradition." He seemed about to add something, but apparently changed his mind.

A moment later they drew up in front of a tall redbrick house set on the banks of the Houghton Brook.

Hardy switched off the engine. "Welcome to Mill House," he announced. "Just in time for the afternoon hatch."

As if on cue, there was a sudden splash as a trout rose not twenty feet from the car.

Powell turned to his host. "Jim," he said, "I think I've died and gone to heaven."

At that moment he could not have known—although he should have known it better than most—that things are not always what they seem.

* * *

A brace of trout fried in lightly seasoned butter and a bottle of Mersault later, Powell sat in Hardy's study in front of a crackling log fire drinking Scotch with his host and reminiscing about their university days. "Well, it's worked out all right for you, Jim," Powell ventured, feeling for his cigarettes.

Hardy shrugged. "Can't complain. Gets a bit lonely at times, but one can't have everything, I suppose." He paused for a moment. "I don't know, there's something about the *predictability* of Houghton Bridge, for want of a better word. It's provided me with a certain stability in my life that I've never had before. I'll spare you the gory details, but my divorce was extremely messy and, well, I'm just happy to have put it all behind me." He leaned over with a light. "And what about you, Erskine? Life as a Scotland Yard detective must be rather exciting, flying around London thwarting villains and whatnot."

"It has its moments. Separated by interminable interludes of sheer bloody boredom."

Hardy smiled knowingly. "I expect the bureaucratic beast requires considerable care and feeding."

"That, Jim, is an understatement of epic proportions." Anxious to steer the conversation along more uplifting lines, he continued, "And speaking of understatement, have I told you that I think the Houghton Brook is the loveliest trout stream I've ever laid eyes on."

"The best piece of dry fly water in the world," Hardy agreed with conviction. He raised his glass. "To Pamela Street—long may she reign." He gulped down his whisky.

Had a shadow flickered across his face just then? "You

mentioned that her husband passed away some years ago," Powell observed casually, probing against his better judgment. "I take it she has remarried."

Hardy eyed his guest thoughtfully. "Shortly after the old boy fell off the perch, she hooked up with an actor named Simon Street. Ever heard of him?"

"Should I have?"

"Not particularly. But don't tell him that. A legend in his own mind, that one. Did some repertory theater, apparently, then had a shot at the big time in the eighties with a play in the West End. Bombed spectacularly, I'm told. Pamela must have taken pity on him, although she no doubt finds it useful to have a man around to help her run the estate."

"You don't sound entirely sold on Mr. Street."

Hardy frowned. "Well, he's a bit of a gigolo, if you ask me. Colonel Waddington was considerably older than Pamela. She was completely devoted to him, by all accounts, but she's an attractive woman—about our age, I should think—and Simon can be very charming if you like the smarmy type. Personally, I can't stand him." He paused. "Am I boring you with all this local gossip?" He had begun to slur his words slightly.

Powell smiled. "Not at all. Gossip is a policeman's stock-in-trade."

Hardy laughed. "An unhealthy interest in one's neighbors' business is an essential ingredient of village life. For sheer entertainment value it beats the telly hands down." He paused, an odd expression on his face. "And believe me, there is plenty of good material to work with in Houghton Bridge." He lapsed into silence and stared into the fire. "The thing is," he said eventually, "if anything ever happened to Pamela . . ." He trailed off pensively.

Hardy's non sequitur caught Powell's attention. "Does she have any children?" he asked.

"No, no children."

Powell finished his drink and set the glass down.

"Here, let me get you another."

Powell suppressed a yawn. "No thank you, Jim. I think I'll turn in. Must be the country air."

Hardy nodded. "I won't be far behind you. Breakfast is served from eight until ten, so I'll see you then. I'd recommend an early start so you can be on the water by ten. You can start above the stile where we finished off this afternoon, then work your way up to the Hatch Pool. It's been fishing well the past few days. I've got to run some errands in Stockbridge and probably won't be back until late in the afternoon. You can pack some sandwiches for lunch or try the pub."

Powell got to his feet with his host following suit. "This is very kind of you, Jim—"

Hardy raised his hand in protest. "Not at all. You'd do the same for me."

After Powell had gone, Hardy walked over to the hearth. He picked up a poker and stabbed at the embers, causing a violent eruption of sparks.

CHAPTER 7

The next morning, despite his auspicious debut with the trout of Houghton Brook the previous afternoon, Powell was not exactly in top form. A gusty downstream wind made casting difficult, and he spent most of his time untying knots in his leader as opposed to actually fishing. This was all the more frustrating since every trout in the stream appeared to be gorging with gay abandon on tiny olive duns, which he was unable to match with anything in his fly box. Even his old standby, the Iron Blue Dun, failed to produce a rise.

At about eleven-thirty he decided to pack it in. He dropped his rod off at the guesthouse, then set out for the pub. He followed the narrow lane they had driven up the day before to where it crossed over the stream. He stopped on the bridge to look back. Off to his right, Mill House was just visible through a leafy lattice of willows, and up on the left, overlooking the little valley, rose the impressive half-timbered facade of Houghton Manor, where, he fancied, the lady of the manor consorted with her faded thespian. Having discarded his walking stick in London, he took his time, although he was limping only slightly now. Ten minutes later he found himself in the public bar of the Mayfly Inn.

The inn, dating from the sixteenth century, was one of two surviving coaching inns that had once competed for the coaching trade in Houghton Bridge. The village lay just to the east of one of the longest and steepest hills in England, where the road climbed out of the Test Valley. Teams of horses were frequently changed there so that fresh animals could be used to tackle the severe grade. Nowadays the Mayfly Inn's claim to fame was as a gathering place for well-heeled anglers who paid exorbitant sums for the privilege of fishing the River Test. It was also the headquarters, Powell knew, for the famous Mayfly Fishing Club.

As he waited for his pint, he glanced around the room. Oak and polished brass and green walls hung with fishing memorabilia—an old creel, a glass-fronted case of flies, and several signed photographs of famous patrons smiling with their catches. And dominating the room above the bar was an enormous stuffed pike armed with a fearsome, if slightly improbable mouthful of teeth. Useful for enforcing closing time, he thought. He ordered a ploughman's, then took a table by a window.

There were several other patrons in the pub: two Americans complaining loudly to each other and anyone else who cared to listen about the lack of fish; a tweedy, ruddy-faced man with a grating voice and an attractive female companion who gave the impression she was bored to death with his company; and a group of elderly couples chatting cheerfully over plates heaped high with fish and chips at several tables along the opposite wall—undoubtedly the occupants of the tour bus parked outside. It struck Powell as he observed the group of seniors, who were obviously enjoying themselves, that people of his parents' generation seemed able to make the best of any situation—he shuddered—even a pensioners' coach tour. Spirit of the Blitz, he supposed. At the table next to him, a pale young man in mud-caked wellies sat alone staring off into space.

Powell demolished his lunch in short order and then glanced at his watch. Time for one more, then a bit of sight-seeing around the village.

"Same again, sir?" asked the balding, middle-aged man behind the bar.

Powell surveyed the row of tap handles. "I think a pint of Gale's this time."

"Right." The man appeared to size him up. "Down for the fishing, are you, sir?"

"Bit of fishing, bit of relaxation," Powell replied.

"Staying in the village, then?"

"Mill House."

"Your first time in Houghton Bridge?"

Powell nodded, wondering when he was going to get his bloody drink.

The publican waited expectantly.

"It's very nice," Powell volunteered.

The man looked slightly miffed. "Yes, well, we like it. That'll be two pounds five, please."

As he made his way back to his seat he couldn't help noticing that the young man at the next table was watching him. Powell smiled and he looked away.

A moment later the telephone jangled behind the bar.

"Brian!" the publican called out. "It's for you."

The young man sprang to his feet.

"You'd better take it in the back," the publican suggested pointedly. Powell could have sworn he was looking at *him* as he spoke.

The Reverend Geoffrey Norris, secateurs in hand, stumped up the steep hill above the car park leading to St. Andrew's Church. When he reached the top, the tall stone tower rising above him against a perfect blue sky and the ranks of weathered gravestones straggling down the grassy slope behind, he paused, as he always did, to reflect on the transcendence of the spirit over the flesh. Then he suddenly frowned, his musings interrupted by an unexpected intrusion of the profane. He bent down and snipped vigorously at an untidy clump of grass that had sprung up amidst the daffodils lining the path. He couldn't imagine how he'd missed it before. Straightening slowly, he wiped his brow with his sleeve. His fleshy face was flushed from the exertion and he couldn't help wondering if the effort required to climb Church Hill was the reason attendance had fallen off in recent years—a deterrence to his increasingly elderly parishioners.

As he walked through the gate, feeling somewhat deflated, he noticed a tall chap standing round the side of the church, gazing intently at something on the ground. He looked to be in his early fifties with graying hair that was a little longer than was fashionable these days. One would not have described him as having an average build, exactly—*solid* was the word that came to mind. The vicar called out a greeting. The man looked up and waved before turning back to the object of his attention.

The Reverend Norris walked over to stand beside the visitor and followed his gaze to the concrete gutter at the base of the drainpipe that ran down the wall of the church. The vicar stood rigidly for several seconds, transfixed.

There, sunning itself in the gutter, was a small snake.

The Reverend Geoffrey Norris offered his guest a biscuit, giving the odd impression that he wasn't entirely accustomed to having visitors for tea at the vicarage. He smiled. "I hope you don't think that the presence of a g-g-garter snake at St. Andrew's signifies anything, er, of a theological nature."

"What a curious idea!" Powell rejoined good-humoredly. "It strikes me that there is more of Elysium than Erebus in Houghton Bridge."

The vicar frowned. "More like heaven than hell, you mean? Yes, well, we do our best." He looked slightly bemused. Then he brightened. "Silly me, I've left the tea things in the kitchen. You must excuse me, Chief Superintendent."

"It's Erskine, please."

The vicar beamed. "And you m-m-must call me Geoffrey!"

As the vicar bustled about the kitchen, Powell took in his surroundings. The vicarage was a functional house, not luxurious, a roof and a home for the vicar, whom he gathered was a bachelor; somewhere to eat, sleep, and say his prayers. There was an upright piano, pastoral prints on the walls, a small TV, and a faint musty smell that reminded him of his grandparents' house. Powell wondered what it would be like to live alone in such a place.

"How long have you been at St. Andrew's?" Powell asked when the vicar returned.

"Nearly twenty years now," he said. "I was born in Nether Wallop, not far from here, and even as a young boy I knew my calling. At the age of nineteen I was rejected at my interview for ordinands on the grounds of immaturity. I wasn't hurt or surprised, I just accepted it and decided to take up gardening as a profession. In many ways tending a garden is very much like m-m-ministering. One labors to nurture the good and the beautiful and to weed out evil, as it were." He smiled. "To cut a long story short, at twenty-eight I offered myself for ordination again and was accepted. I attended Bishop's College in Winchester and after two curacies wound up at St. Andrew's in nineteen eighty-two. I've been here ever s-s-since, tending to my flock, as it were. Did you know that the original church dates back to Saxon times?" He frowned thoughtfully. "I don't know quite how to put it, but being a part of something so—so *old,* I suppose—gives one a comforting sense of continuity." He looked at Powell apologetically. "You must excuse me—I do tend to go on."

Powell smiled. "Not at all. It must be a very rewarding life."

The vicar seemed to consider this suggestion carefully. "Yes, yes I suppose it is. I've never married, Erskine, but strange as it may sound, I've rarely felt lonely or hard done by. In fact, the church has been the making of me. Did you know that I used to s-stutter terribly? But it's got so much better that people don't deem to notice anymore."

Powell feigned a look of surprise.

The vicar continued. "I think accepting responsibility for the well-being of others is a tremendously liberating experience; it takes one's mind off one's own small problems. I'm the first to admit that I'm neither an intellectual nor a theologian. Nor, I hasten to add, am I a saint, but I try in my own small way to make the world a b-better place. That's all any of us can do when it comes right down to it. D-don't you agree?"

As Powell retraced his steps down Church Hill he reflected on his conversation with the Reverend Geoffrey Norris. He concluded that the clergyman's air of sincerity and—for want of a better word—innocence made him a formidable confessor. During his brief visit with the vicar, Powell realized that he had unwittingly revealed much of his own life story and probably a few other things besides. It also occurred to him that they were both, each in his own way, very much concerned with death and decay, which in the one case served to corroborate faith, in the other to corrode it.

Thus preoccupied and sorely in need of spiritual fortification, Powell found himself once again in the High Street.

CHAPTER 8

The High Street of Houghton Bridge, which dated from Roman times, was basically a broad causeway of packed chalk once used by Welsh drovers to drive their cattle to market in Winchester. It was lined with tidy Georgian houses and color-washed shops that catered increasingly to a growing population of upscale urban refugees and, during the fishing season, to visitors. Powell strolled down the pavement in the afternoon sun taking in the sights—past the Peking Duck and the premises of "W. Sykes, High-Class Family Butcher," and one or two tourist traps of the Ye Olde Shoppe variety. He stepped into the news agent's for some cigarettes and a local paper, then crossed the street, dodging the postman on his bicycle, and made a beeline for the Coach and Horses, which he had sussed out earlier.

The Coach and Horses provided a stark contrast to the gentrified ambience of the Mayfly Inn—it was all dark beams and dingy corners, with a flashing, beeping pinball

machine and a tiny television set blaring tinnily above the
bar. There was no sign of any food on offer and, judging
by the demeanor of the few locals in attendance, it was obviously a place for serious drinking. Powell ordered a pint
of real ale and a packet of crisps from the cadaverous-
looking landlord, then took a seat by the window where
he could read his newspaper and watch the comings and
goings in the street.

He had just settled into his paper, when a man burst
into the pub demanding a gin and tonic.

"Make it a very large one, Harry," he boomed in a
deep, fruity voice. *"Thus far our fortune keeps an upward
course, and we are graced with wreaths of victory!"*

"Celebrating, are we, Mr. Street?" the publican inquired.

"You could say that, Harry. You could certainly say
that."

"Got the part, then?"

Street stared at the innkeeper. "Got the part? The
bloody play was written for me." He spoke deliberately,
condescendingly, as if to make sure he was under-
stood.

"Is that a fact?" the publican replied, stifling a yawn.

Street scowled and threw himself into the nearest chair.
He appeared to size up his audience as he polished off his
drink. A youth about twenty slumped in his chair at the
next table, too drunk to hold his head up; beside him, his
girlfriend carried on a conversation with herself; a couple
of yobs glared at him from the corner; and Powell ignored
him, reading his paper. Street's attention returned to the

girl and he examined her speculatively. She attempted a queasy smile, then belched impressively. Street grimaced. Having no doubt concluded that he was playing to a tough house, he got to his feet and strolled to the door with studied nonchalance. "Philistines," he muttered as he went out.

"And you're a bleeding arsehole," the publican remarked to no one in particular.

Powell got up and walked over to the bar for another pint. "That wouldn't be Simon Street of Houghton Manor, by any chance?" he asked.

The publican's eyes narrowed. "That's 'im, all right. But the question is, who are you, mate?"

Powell introduced himself and explained in an easy manner that he was staying at Mill House with his friend Jim Hardy, who had filled him in on some of the local color.

The landlord seemed satisfied with this explanation. "Jim's all right," he said. "He's competition, in a manner of speaking, but you could say we cater to a different clientele." He laughed, but it sounded more like a paroxysm of wheezing.

Powell smiled and lit a cigarette. "Tell me, Mr. . . ."

"Harry. 'Ere, give us a fag, would you? I'm trying to quit, but a bloke's got to live, 'asn't he?"

"Truer words were never spoken, Harry." Powell offered him a cigarette. "Tell me, does Mr. Street come here often?"

The innkeeper bristled. "You don't think the Coach and Horses is good enough for the likes of 'im, is that it?"

Powell smiled. "Not at all. In fact, I doubt that he would appreciate the quality of your beer. It's just that, well, he didn't seem entirely at ease. . . ."

Harry snorted. "He's a fucking snob, that's why. If you're not in the magic circle, 'e won't give you the time of day. 'E only graces us with 'is presence because 'e's afraid to show 'is face in the Mayfly."

Powell raised an eyebrow. "Really?"

Harry grinned. "Yeah, rumor is the bugger got caught poaching on the club water. Around 'ere that's in the same category as rape and murder."

"You don't say. I'll have another Beckett's, please."

"Right."

One of the yobs lumbered up to the bar, eyed Powell blearily, and then muttered something unintelligible. Harry opened two cans of lager and sent him on his way.

Powell took a sip of his beer. "I'm wondering about something, Harry. Why would Street risk his reputation by poaching? I thought he had his own fishing on the Houghton Brook."

" 'E does, or rather *she* does." He winked slyly. "Story goes there was a big old trout living below the bridge that marks the boundary between the Manor's water and the Mayfly Club's. Seems old Simon was fishing just upstream of the bridge one day and let his fly drift down under the bridge into the club water and snagged the old bugger." He wheezed noisily, whether as a result of mirth or cigarette smoke, Powell was unable to say.

When he had regained his composure, the innkeeper continued. "It's all about competition, mate—one-upmanship. The thing is, I can put up with the toffs in the Mayfly Club—at least you knows where you stands with them. It's Street and 'is like I can't stomach. 'E's no better than you and me but 'e ponces around 'ere like Lord Muck."

Powell nodded sympathetically and finished his pint. Jim was right, he thought—for sheer entertainment value, village gossip beats the telly hands down. "Well, Harry, I must run. I'll pop by again."

The innkeeper looked skeptical. "Cheers, mate."

It rained that evening, so Powell stayed in after dinner. The other guests had settled in for the night and Powell sat with Hardy in his study, recounting his experience at the Coach and Horses.

"I've heard the same story, but I don't put much stock in it," Hardy said. "Street may be many things, most of them exceedingly unpleasant, but I don't believe he's an idiot. He probably has other reasons for avoiding the Mayfly."

"Such as?"

Hardy shrugged. "Your guess is as good as mine."

"I wonder what his wife would do if she found out that old Simon had been poaching on the Mayfly Club water," Powell mused.

"I'm sure she'd be absolutely mortified. She'd no doubt view it as a stain on the Waddington escutcheon—" he hesitated "—but it's difficult to say what she'd do about it. I mean, I'm sure she'd give him a severe bollocking at least."

"But she must have heard the story—I've only been here two days and I already know all about it."

"Difficult to say. Mrs. Street is held in the highest regard in Houghton Bridge, and one must bear in mind that it *is* only a rumor. Even if it were true, I for one would never dream of mentioning it to her."

"When did this alleged incident occur?"

Hardy looked at him. "Do I detect a certain Sherlockian interest in your tone? The Mystery of the Missing Trout," he intoned melodramatically.

Powell smiled sheepishly. "Force of habit, I suppose."

"To answer your question, it supposedly happened seven or eight years ago. I'd been here a couple of years and it was just before—" He checked himself. "Anyway, it was a long time ago."

A sudden gust of wind rattled the windowpane, and the two men lapsed into silence.

Powell felt strangely on edge. Here he was on holiday in a charming B&B with a congenial host on one of the best trout streams in the country, yet he found himself unable to unwind. He had promised himself that for the next few days he would think of nothing but fishing, but he couldn't help wondering if his domestic crisis wasn't at the root of his malaise. Or perhaps, at a more mundane level, it was simply the prospect of returning to work to face Merriman. In any case, his penchant for poking his nose into other people's business to avoid having to deal with his own problems was pathetically transparent. Getting right down to it, this was probably the reason he had become a policeman in the first place. He decided that the profundity of this particular insight called for another drink.

He emptied his glass and attempted to catch Hardy's attention. However, his friend was staring into the fire, preoccupied with his own thoughts.

CHAPTER 9

Danica Hughes fiddled with her spoon as she waited in the restaurant in Stockbridge the next morning. She looked out the window at a gray day and an even grayer prospect. The downs were shrouded in low clouds, creating a feeling of claustrophobia. Now that she thought about it, it was a complete mystery why she had agreed to meet him in the first place. Nothing he could do or say would change the way she felt; he could only make things worse. She suddenly experienced a sense of foreboding, a vague feeling of dread that was unfocused but nonetheless palpable. It was as if her life were spinning out of control under the influence of some sinister conjunction of planets.

When she had first learned shortly after her own arrival that Richard Garrett was returning to Houghton Bridge, she had been unable to dismiss it as mere coincidence. And even when she heard that he had been nominated for membership in the club—which would explain why he would want to put in an appearance, like a politician campaigning for election—she still couldn't help wondering about his motives. According to Brian, it was the first time he had been back since Maggie's death.

She had never liked Garrett and, superficialities aside, could never understand what Maggie had seen in him. When she had asked her father about him, the old river-keeper had been characteristically diplomatic. But then what had she expected? The Mayfly Club looks after its own.

She tried to pass the time by watching the other patrons, but she felt her mind being pulled down into a whirlpool of memories, and once again she found herself asking the question she had asked a thousand times before. What if she had agreed to meet Maggie that day instead of worrying about her own selfish needs? What if she hadn't gone to meet John and—she dropped her spoon with a clatter as if to distract herself. She rubbed her temples to ease the throbbing. She knew she shouldn't have come. She rummaged through her bag for an aspirin, took a sip of tepid tea, and tossed her head back to swallow it. She was just about to gather up her things and leave, when she heard his voice behind her.

"Hello, Dani. Sorry I'm late."

She twisted in her chair and glared at him. "Don't you ever call me that." He was just as she remembered him, impossibly good-looking and only too aware of it.

Garrett smiled easily. "I'd forgotten. That's what Maggie used to call you, isn't it? I'm sorry."

She said nothing.

"Do you mind if I sit down?"

"I was just leaving," she said.

"But I've come all this way and I wouldn't want you to leave angry."

"Don't patronize me, Richard. Sit down if you must. I'll give you five minutes, so make the best of it."

He pulled up a chair and sat across from her. "You haven't changed a bit, Danica."

"Haven't I?"

"Still as beautiful as ever."

"Fuck off, Richard."

A look of mock indignation. "Danica, really!"

"Times have changed, Richard. I'm not the river-keeper's daughter anymore, so I don't have to bow and scrape to you. Now let's get this over with. Why did you call me?"

"It's obvious, isn't it? I'd heard you'd come back and I just wanted to see how you were getting on."

She regarded him coldly. "You always were a good liar."

His expression turned serious. "I know how close you and Maggie were, how hard you took her suicide—"

Her eyes flashed. "I don't think it *was* a suicide." Her voice raised and heads were turning in the restaurant.

Garrett looked startled. "Danica, I—"

"And even if it was, we all know who was responsible, don't we?"

He regarded her without speaking for several moments, then got to his feet. "I'm sorry you feel that way. You really have no idea, do you?"

She did not reply.

"Good-bye, Danica."

She watched him as he walked out.

After returning from tea at the vicarage, Pamela Street sat in the library at Houghton Manor, attempting to arrange a bouquet of flowers in a crystal vase. She had picked them along the edge of the water meadow on the way home, thinking they would look lovely in the library. She had tried all the permutations and combinations she could think of—the yellow ones in front (what *were* the yellow ones called?) or in a ring around the outside like a golden crown or scattered evenly throughout—but nothing looked right. Eventually she gave up and gathered them all together in an untidy bunch and stuffed them in the vase, scattering pink and yellow petals on the desk.

She leaned back in her chair and closed her eyes. She lost track of time but when she opened her eyes, sunlight was pouring into the room through the window, illuminating the multicolored spines of the books on the shelves like a mosaic of stained glass. She thought about her late husband, Leslie, and how he used to discard the dust wrappers from his books, believing that they were a garish marketing ploy that obscured the bookbinder's art—the restful combination of green, brown, red, and blue leather that surrounded her now. She used to scold him about this harmless eccentricity because it reduced the value of his collection, but he would always answer that he had no intention of ever selling them, so it really didn't matter. It was at moments like this she missed him most and longed for his reassuring presence. He had always known what to say or do in any situation.

She began to gather up the petals in an agitated manner. Leslie would never have allowed the financial position of the estate to deteriorate so badly; she had no head for figures herself, and Simon was—well, he was just Simon. She was naturally concerned about her own future, but there were so many others who depended on her and she couldn't bear the thought of letting them down. But just when she needed to really think things through, she found it difficult to concentrate on even the simplest tasks—

She suddenly started, her body rigid. There was someone moving in the hall. "Who's there?" she called out in a brittle voice. "Simon, is that you?"

Simon Street swept into the room bearing a tray with two glasses and a sheaf of papers. "Who else would it be, my sweet?" He studied her critically. "You look like you've just seen a ghost." He raised an eyebrow. "Been chatting with Leslie again, have we?" He walked over to the desk and set the tray down. "I've brought you a G and T to settle your nerves. Just what the doctor ordered."

Pamela, clutching the glass with both hands, gulped down the contents.

"That's the ticket." He handed her the other glass. "You have mine—it's still a bit early for me." He watched with satisfaction as she made short work of it as well. "Feeling better now?"

She nodded numbly.

He relieved her of the glass, then sat down across the

desk from her and spread the papers out in front of him. "Now then, I've had a look at the books and I don't wish to worry you needlessly, but we really should review your assets to make sure you're realizing the maximum return on investment. Expenses have done nothing but go up over the past few years, yet the estate's income has remained relatively static. Take the staff, for instance. Can you really afford two full-time gardeners?"

She took a moment to digest this. "Mr. and Mrs. Hobson have been with me for years. I couldn't let either one of them go."

Street affected an air of long-suffering patience. "What about the fishing, then? You let your best water to the Mayfly Club and that freeloader at Mill House. At least the club pays for the privilege—albeit a fraction of market value. But Hardy is simply taking advantage of your good nature."

She shook her head stubbornly. "It was Colonel Waddington's wish—"

He slammed his fist on the desk, causing her to start. "Sod Colonel Waddington! Haven't you been listening to a word I've said?" He raised his voice to a crescendo. "If you don't do something, Pamela, you'll lose Houghton Manor, the estate, everything you've worked for all your life."

She stared at him transfixed, unable to speak.

He reached over and patted her hand, his voice soothing now. "In fact, Pamela, I think you should seriously consider selling Houghton Manor now, when you can do it on your own terms, as opposed to waiting until things get much worse and you're forced to let it go at a boot sale price. Leslie wouldn't want that to happen, now would he?"

She shook her head numbly.

Street smiled. "That's better." He stood up and walked around behind her. He began to massage her shoulders. "Did I tell you I've received a very attractive offer from an American fishing tackle firm—the one that owns the shop in Stockbridge? Chalk stream fishing commands a top price these days, and there is no shortage of rich Americans lining up for the privilege." He paused to let this register. "Just think, Pamela, we could live anywhere we wanted in London and start enjoying life. The theater every night, the best restaurants, friends who don't have cow shit on their boots." He felt her muscles tighten, so he pressed harder with his fingers. "I've got to pop up to London next week to see about the play. Why don't you come with me? We can see your solicitor and arrange everything."

She knew better than to argue when he was like this, spouting his grandiose schemes. "I wonder what I'd do without you, Simon," she said in a flat voice.

He traced his forefinger down the nape of her neck and felt her shudder. "Don't you worry about anything, my sweet. Simon will take care of you."

CHAPTER 10

Brian Stewart, nature warden for the Houghton Bridge Conservancy Area, leaned on his spade and surveyed his handiwork. The little ditch he had opened up off the main carrier stream ran freely again. The water was murky after passing through the freshly dug section, but it would soon clear up. The meadow was shrouded in morning mist and the usual chorus of birdsong was strangely absent. The only sounds were his ragged breathing and the whisper of flowing water.

The water meadow was essentially an elaborate irrigation system consisting of an artificial network of ridges and channels fed by water from the Houghton Brook. A weir across the stream diverted water into a head main or carrier. The water was in turn led from the main into a network of progressively shallower and narrower carriers set at right angles to the main and aligned with the gradient of the meadow. The water flowed into the carriers through a series of sluices, fitted with adjustable gates or

71

hatches, to ensure an even distribution of water over the meadow. Once the water had spilled from the carriers it flowed across the plots on which the grass grew and into drains, which got progressively wider and deeper, finally leading into a tail drain on the lowest ground, which carried the water back into the River Test on the other side of the village.

Historically, the water meadow at Houghton Bridge (and countless others like it on the chalk downlands) was flooded in the early spring to provide pasture for the lambs and ewes at a time when other food was scarce. Later in the summer it was flooded again to produce a hay crop and was then used for cattle grazing until late in the year when the channels were cleared and the hatches repaired. In use from the seventeenth century onward, the number of active water meadows declined in the nineteenth century because they were too costly and labor-intensive to operate.

The surviving water meadow at Houghton Bridge was supported by a grant from the Countryside Commission, and Brian Stewart, employed part-time by the local council, spent his days tinkering with the water distribution system—repairing a weir here, adjusting a sluice gate there, and generally maintaining the fifty or so acres of common meadow for the enjoyment of the villagers and the few cattle and sheep that still grazed there. He knew every square foot of ground; he knew the name of every bird and flower, insect and animal that frequented the meadow. He knew it in every season and in all its moods.

He sometimes thought about the water meadow as a metaphor for his own life. Its continued existence against all odds created the impression of stability, like the annual spawning cycle of the trout in Houghton Brook. But he knew that this was an illusion. The stream was polluted with agricultural runoff, and much of its flow was now being drained off to supply vast housing estates that were invading the countryside like a cancer, just like the stocked rainbow trout from America were displacing the wild brown trout.

Since Maggie's death he had settled into a routine that was designed to avoid thinking, decisions, responsibility, or anything else remotely associated with the exercise of free will. He had long ago given up any thoughts of writing and now spent his days keeping busy outdoors and his evenings in the pub, exploring the twists and turns of the River Lethe as he liked to think of it. He had got used to living alone and had managed to achieve a measure of— if not equanimity—at least equilibrium in his life.

But all that had changed the day Dani came home. She was a constant and painful reminder of what once had been and, even more wrenching for Stewart, what might have been. It was not as if he hadn't thought about her every day for the past seven years, dreamed about the day she would return to Houghton Bridge; it was rather that he never really believed it would happen. Easy then to fantasize about a future where love would rise like a phoenix from the ashes of his shattered life and they would both live happily ever after in their rose-covered cottage. But as he thought about it now, he was disgusted with himself for having indulged in such cloying sentimentality.

And then there was the unexpected appearance of Richard Garrett to contend with—the man he held responsible for his sister's death. Why hadn't the bastard been content to leave well enough alone and just stay away? Stewart's expression hardened.

A sudden gust of wind sprang up, worrying the willows along the stream. Stewart turned up his jacket collar and shouldered his spade. He looked up at the ambiguous gray sky for guidance. Take your medication, they'd told him, and everything will be all right.

Except it wouldn't be all right—he knew that. He knew it as well as he knew every ridge and furrow in his water meadow.

Mrs. Emily Iverson, it could fairly be said, was an enthusiast. As she crept along the path, skirting the water meadow, binoculars at the ready, her spry and lively manner belied her eighty-three years. An avid birder, she took every opportunity to pursue her hobby—if a lifelong dedication to the advancement of ornithological science could be dismissed as a mere hobby. Since retiring as the village postmistress over twenty years ago, she had set off along the river path every morning at precisely nine o'clock, starting at the Test Bridge, walking along the river and the Houghton Brook, and finishing up at the Mayfly Inn an hour or so later. Then back at her cottage, over her second cup of tea, she would record her detailed observations in her journal.

Even the gray and dreary weather that prevailed that particular morning did not dampen her spirits. On the contrary, she considered conditions that would normally be considered adverse for birding a challenge to be overcome by her acute powers of observation. She was only halfway along on her walk and she had already chalked up a cuckoo, a pale blue kingfisher, a reed warbler on its nest and, most gratifying of all, a little dipper, which alternated its time between bobbing up and down on top of a moss-covered rock and walking submerged along the bottom of the Houghton Brook in search of insects.

The stillness was broken occasionally by the croak of a moorhen, and as she made her way quietly along the Houghton Brook, Mrs. Iverson was determined to catch a glimpse of the shy bird and its young ones. She reckoned they must be just up ahead near the weir where the main carrier left the stream, a little beyond where she had last seen them yesterday.

The path swung to the right at this point and crossed the main carrier about a hundred feet away from the Houghton Brook, which was obscured by a screen of trees. When she reached the carrier she followed it back up toward the stream. Just as she was about to begin her final stalk, there was a sudden explosion of wings as a gaudy cock pheasant clattered into the air from underfoot. Mrs. Iverson, uttering a word that would later cause her to blush when she recalled the incident, realized that the startled pheasant had flown over the stream at precisely the point where she had expected to encounter her quarry. She stood still for several minutes and, confirming her worst fears, there wasn't another peep from the moorhen.

She was debating what to do next—whether to continue on her walk or wait there in the faint hope the moorhen would return—when she noticed something peculiar about the carrier flowing beside her. It was about two feet wide and a foot deep at this point, and the water had a slight rusty tinge to it. She frowned. That's odd, she thought. Always on the alert for pollution and other environmental insults on her patch, she decided she had better investigate. She followed the carrier toward its source, noticing that the rusty coloration was getting more pronounced.

As she neared the Houghton Brook her eyes were drawn to the sluice gate that controlled the flow into the carrier. She blinked uncomprehendingly. There was something caught under the heavy iron gate.

She gasped. It was a man, or rather a man's head. Water gushed over and around him, his hair plastered to his face, eyes wide and staring. Blood ran freely from his nostrils and mouth, staining the water red.

Mrs. Iverson sat down unceremoniously on the path as if she were staging a protest. "Oh, my goodness!" she said.

CHAPTER 11

Powell cursed his clumsiness as he crouched awkwardly on the bank of the Houghton Brook watching a sizable trout feeding about twenty feet upstream. The weather was a little on the cool side for mayflies, so he had tied on his old favorite, a number 16 Iron Blue Dun, which seemed about the same size as the little olives that were hatching sporadically. However, his first attempt to cover the fish had resulted in his leader and fly falling on the water in an untidy heap a yard short of the trout, which turned out to be a blessing in disguise. For had the whole mess landed directly on top of the trout, it would likely have sent it scurrying for cover, never to be seen again.

Powell tried to discern the trout's exact whereabouts. He knew it was lying near the far bank of the stream a few feet downstream of a leaning hawthorn tree. He searched the pebbled bottom where he had last seen the fish rise but there was no sign of it. Admittedly, the flat gray light was not conducive to underwater visibility; however, the

water was less than three feet deep and he knew he must
be staring right at the fish, unable to interpret the visual
clues in front of his nose.

Suddenly a fly popped out onto the surface of the
water just above the hawthorn and began to float downstream with the current, its wings set stoically like the
miniature mainsail of a doomed sloop entering the
Bermuda Triangle. As Powell watched, a long undulating
shadow resolved itself in the exact spot where he had been
looking and rose toward the surface like a languid torpedo.
The trout intercepted the insect with the precision of a
surface-to-air missile, engulfed it with an audible *slurp,*
and then sounded, providing a glimpse of a broad speckled
back before miraculously disappearing once again.

With fumbling fingers Powell checked the knot on his
fly. He considered the position. The trout was obviously
receptive, having taken every natural fly that had floated
over him in the last ten minutes. The operation was, in
theory at least, relatively straightforward. All he had to do
was float his artificial fly over the fish without frightening
it half to death. The trick was to drop the fly on the water
with a minimum amount of disturbance at a point upstream of the hawthorn, but as close to it as possible without getting caught up in its branches. In an ideal world, he
would have preferred to cast well upstream to avoid any
possibility of entanglement with the tree; however, the
presence of a half-submerged fence post two or three
yards above the hawthorn precluded this approach. Then
once the fly was safely on water, let it float downstream
with the current, completely free of any unnatural drag

from the line, into the trout's field of vision—which is a
subject of some considerable complexity in its own right.

Due to the different refractive properties of air and water,
light bends when it penetrates the water, creating a rather
curious effect for both the fish and the fisherman. Contrary
to what one might expect, the surface of the water appears
to the trout as a mirror, reflecting back the pebbles and
weeds of the stream bottom. However, if the fish looks directly overhead it sees a small round window, through
which the world beyond the stream—the sky, the trees, or
someone standing on the bank waving a fishing rod
about—is clearly revealed.

All of this has important implications for the angler
stalking his quarry. First of all, he or she must stay out of
sight by crouching down so as not to be seen through the
fish's window. Secondly, he must use an artificial fly that
looks like the genuine article. In order to simulate nature
as closely as possible, he fashions his flies from the very
stiffest feathers taken from the neck of a rooster specially
bred for the purpose, so that the individual fibers prick
and dimple the surface of the trout's mirrored ceiling like
the legs and tail of a living insect. This alerts the fish to
the presence of a potential meal. Then, as the fly enters
the window and the trout rises to have a closer look, it
must endure the closest scrutiny, more rigorous than that
of any entomology student. It must be the correct size and
color, the wings must sit upright, and it must sit naturally
in the surface film. For the angler this is all a pleasant di-
version, but for the trout it is a game of life and death.

Although such conscious considerations were the furthest

thing from Powell's mind that morning, he nonetheless took them into account as he considered his approach. Try as he might, he could see no flaw in his plan of attack.

He took a deep breath and began to work out a length of line, keeping his rod low over the water and under the trout's radar. Piece of cake, he tried to reassure himself. When he had about twenty feet of line in the air, he flicked his rod forward smartly and watched the leader and fly unfurl before settling neatly around the fence post.

Cursing violently, he wagged his rod tip ineffectually back and forth in an attempt to dislodge the fly, which was hooked over the leader, forming a sort of lasso around the post. He had to keep the line fairly taut as he did so in order to avoid causing a commotion in the water and frightening his quarry, but this constraint rather defeated the purpose of the exercise. In a last-ditch effort, he flipped a large loop of line upstream, which created sufficient slack to enable the leader and fly to slip down the post into the water.

Miraculously the hook came free of the leader and the fly began to drift, half-drowned but still floating, under the hawthorn. Powell held his breath as the giant trout, clearly visible now, detached itself from the bottom and rose to inspect his fly. The fish drifted downstream with the current for several feet, its critical nose scarcely an inch under Powell's offering. Then with a sudden splash it turned and swam away, leaving only the memory of a disdainful wagging tail.

Feeling somewhat deflated—not exactly the state of mind he had anticipated when he'd embarked on his jolly country holiday—Powell collected his kit and headed back to Mill House. To top it all off, when he arrived just before noon he met one of the other guests returning with a fine brace of trout. He eventually found Jim Hardy in the kitchen sitting and staring out the window when he should have been busy preparing lunch. Hardy looked up, his face pale and worried. He spoke in a flat voice, scarcely audible. "There's been a murder," he said.

Powell set about extracting what details he could.

Hardy was shaking his head. "I just can't believe it. Not in Houghton Bridge."

"You did say that village life was more diverting than the telly," Powell remarked.

His host stared at him in disbelief. "This is hardly a joking matter."

"I'm sorry, Jim. That was insensitive of me. Put it down to a policeman's defense mechanism."

Hardy looked contrite. "I'm the one who should apologize. I didn't stop to think that you have to deal with this sort of thing every day."

Powell smiled thinly. "Not quite every day." He neglected to add that he wouldn't mind, though, knowing that this would likely be misinterpreted. "Did you know the victim?" he asked.

"Only slightly. His father is a member of the Mayfly Fishing Club—Bernard Garrett is his name. He's a well-known London solicitor. By all accounts young Richard was destined to follow in his footsteps. As a matter of fact, I understand he'd been nominated for membership in the club this year."

Hardy's brief account sounded like something you'd read in the obits, and Powell got the curious impression that he was holding something back. "Tell me more about the Mayfly Club," he prompted.

Hardy went on to explain what he knew about the club and its membership. "I understand whenever there is a vacancy, three names are put forward for election by the other members. Rumor has it the competition can get quite keen."

"Really? Do you know the other candidates?"

Hardy shook his head. "If you want to know more, I suggest you talk to Sir Robert Alderson. He's the club secretary and seems like a decent chap."

Powell made a mental note. "How did you hear about it?"

"From my housekeeper, Mrs. Fielding. Her friend Mrs. Iverson rang her this morning. When Mrs. Fielding arrived at about eleven she told me."

"Mrs. Iverson?"

"The lady who discovered the body."

"I see. And where exactly was the body found?"

"On the Houghton Brook near the main weir. Stuck in a hatchway, apparently." Hardy went on to explain about the carrier and the system of sluices. Then he described exactly how Mrs. Iverson had found the body.

"Tell me, Jim, have you spoken to the police about this?"

Hardy frowned. "No, why do you ask?"

"When I came in you said there had been a murder. How do you know it wasn't just an unfortunate accident? Maybe he fell into the stream while fishing and got caught up in the sluiceway somehow."

Hardy looked slightly startled by this suggestion. "I don't see how—I mean, the gate was jammed down on his neck. . . ."

Powell considered this for a moment. "Well, that's it, then. I'm sure the local police will take matters in hand. Er, who did you say the local constable was?"

"What? Oh, Constable Bailey." He got to his feet. "You'll have to excuse me, Erskine, I should really be getting back to work. Will you be taking lunch?"

Powell shook his head. "Don't worry about me. I've got some errands to run in the village, so I'll just grab something at the pub."

As Powell set off for Houghton Bridge he felt curiously energized. It did not escape him that he felt most alive when he was embroiled in the misfortune and misery of others. What *did* escape him for the moment were common sense and good judgment, not to mention the likely consequences of sticking his nose in where it didn't belong.

CHAPTER 12

Inspector Andrew Marsh of the Hampshire CID in Andover regarded the local constable with considerable irritation. He had only just arrived in Houghton Bridge—nearly two hours after the fact, as it turned out—after having canceled a much-needed appointment with his dentist. "How is it, Bailey," he asked acidly, "that I wasn't notified until more than an hour after the body was discovered by Mrs.—what's her bloody name?"

PC Bailey affected a cowed demeanor. "Iverson, sir," he replied meekly.

Marsh glared at him. "You'd better explain yourself."

"Well, sir, I thought it was important to, er, secure the scene first—"

"Secure the bloody scene!" Marsh thundered. "If you don't watch your step, my lad, I'll see to it that you finish out your career directing tourists at the local roundabout!"

"Yes, sir."

"Do you realize that valuable evidence may have been

lost or destroyed as a result of your—I'll be generous—
enthusiasm?"

PC Bailey wisely resisted the urge to argue. "Yes, sir."

Marsh winced and sucked on the offending tooth. "I
want you to take me up there for a look round. The scene-
of-crime lads should be there by now. Who's in charge, by
the way?"

"Sergeant Potter from Stockbridge, sir."

Marsh nodded. "I know him. Good man," he added,
followed by a significant pause. "Well?"

"Sir?"

Inspector Marsh sprang to his feet. "What in God's
name are you waiting for, Bailey? I haven't got all day."

The shortest route to the weir on the Houghton Brook
was to take the turning at the Mayfly Inn, park at the bridge,
and then walk back on the path about a hundred yards or so.
It occurred to PC Bailey as he led the way along the path
that Inspector Marsh had not spoken a single word to him
since they had left the police station. This was an ominous
sign, since the young constable's strategy up until this point
was to create a role for himself in the investigation. After
all, how often did a murder occur in the sleepy village of
Houghton Bridge? And PC Bailey had already come to the
conclusion that this was no mere accident.

He glanced up at the sky. The clouds had begun to dis-
sipate and a watery blotch of light overhead presaged a
better day ahead. He could only hope for a corresponding
thaw in his superior's attitude. Up ahead he could hear the
murmur of voices and as he crossed over the carrier and

turned right toward the Houghton Brook, the familiar shape of Sergeant Potter hove into view.

"What kept you, my lad, has—ah, Inspector Marsh, glad you could make it, sir."

"Better late than never, Potter," Marsh snapped as he barged ahead of PC Bailey. "Now then, what's up?"

"Well, sir, it looks like foul play all right."

He led the way through the trees to the sluice gate. The body had not been moved although the main weir just downstream in the Houghton Brook had been opened to lower the water level so that water no longer spilled into the carrier. The police photographer and a fingerprint man bustled purposefully about, snapping and dusting.

Inspector Marsh grimaced as he took in the scene and absently rubbed his jaw. "Bloody marvelous," he remarked. "What do you make of it, Potter?"

"Come see for yourself, sir."

PC Bailey tried not to look at the victim's face, but found his eyes drawn there nonetheless. There was blood everywhere, and the scene appeared decidedly gorier when the water was shut off. He felt his lunch burning in his throat and he forced himself to look away. He was used to attending road accidents, terrible ones sometimes, but this was different. Someone had purposely taken a man's life in the most unpleasant, cold-blooded fashion. He was beginning to wonder if he was cut out for serious crime investigations.

"See here, Mr. Marsh," Sergeant Bailey was saying as he pointed to the mechanism that raised and lowered the gate. "There's an iron ratchet operated by a lever."

"Where's the lever?"

"Over there, sir." He pointed to a labeled plastic bag on the ground containing what appeared to be a rusty iron bar about two feet long.

Marsh walked over and nudged it with his foot. "Was the bar fitted into the winding mechanism at the time the body was discovered?" Sergeant Potter began to answer, but Marsh raised his hand. He looked at PC Bailey. "Well, Bailey? I believe it was you who *secured the scene,* was it not?"

PC Bailey swallowed hard. He stared at the bar. "I-I don't think so, sir. I could check my notebook. . . ."

Marsh sighed heavily. "Potter?"

"The bar was lying on the ground, just as you see it, sir, covered with blood."

"Bagged and labeled, to boot. Bloody considerate of our villain, wouldn't you say?"

Sergeant Potter suppressed the urge to crack a smile and was relieved to see that his young constable had the good sense to do the same.

"Where's the police surgeon?" Marsh asked irritably.

"Dr. Wilson has been and gone, sir, but if you want to talk to him I can—"

"It can wait. Did he offer an opinion on the cause of death?"

"Blow to the head from behind, then he reckons his assailant maneuvered him into position in the sluice and lowered the gate on his neck to finish him off."

Marsh frowned. "Seems a bit excessive, don't you think? I understand the body was discovered around nine-thirty. Did the good doctor come to any conclusions on the time of death?"

"An hour or two earlier, give or take."

Marsh nodded. He looked at the victim's face, a grisly portrait framed in concrete and rusted metal.

"Poor bloke looks like he's been put in stocks," Sergeant Potter remarked.

Marsh looked at him. "Yes, Potter, but what was his crime?"

Sergeant Potter did not answer.

"Do we know his name?"

"Yes, sir. Richard Garrett. He was down for the fishing."

"Is that what he was doing at the time?"

"Looks like it. A trout rod was found lying on the stream bank a few yards away."

"Any leads?"

"Not yet, sir."

Marsh suddenly looked preoccupied. "Garrett . . . that name rings a bell. Not the London solicitor, by any chance?"

"That would be the victim's father, Bernard Garrett."

Marsh winced. "Take my word for it, Potter, this is going to be a juicy one. Now somebody get me a bloody aspirin!"

The Coach and Horses appeared exactly as Powell had left it the day before. The tattooed yobs were still glowering in the corner behind the pinball machine, and the besotted Romeo and his dyspeptic Juliet occupied their usual table at the front.

"Hello, Harry," Powell said as he pulled up a stool at the bar.

The landlord grinned. "Well, well, if it isn't Captain Curiosity. What'll it be?"

"Surprise me."

Harry drew a half of bitter and placed it in front of Powell. "I expect you've 'eard about the murder," he ventured casually.

Powell took a lingering sip of his beer. "Very nice. Has there been a murder?" he asked innocently.

Harry eyed him suspiciously. "Up at 'Oughton Brook this morning. I thought everybody'd 'eard by now."

"Well, Harry, I don't get out much." He drained his glass. "This is really very good. I think I'll have a pint this time and then you can tell me all about it."

Harry looked miffed. "I wouldn't want to bore you."

"And have a very large one for yourself while you're at it."

The landlord grunted and fetched a pint for Powell, then poured himself a whisky.

Powell lit a cigarette and offered one to Harry, who took it with shaking fingers.

The landlord lowered his voice in a conspiratorial tone. "Thanks, guv, you're a real gent." He glanced over his shoulder. "But not a word to the trouble and strife. She thinks I've quit."

Powell winked. "Your secret is safe with me. Now then, what's this about a murder?"

Harry could hardly contain himself. "Up at the weir,

first thing this morning. That busybody, old lady Iverson, found 'im, 'is head jammed under a sluice gate."

Powell looked impressed. "Sounds nasty."

Harry leaned in closer. "Some might say 'e 'ad it coming," he said.

"Really? Did you know the victim?"

" 'Is name's Richard Garrett. Father's a member of the fishing club—big shot London lawyer. Perhaps you've 'eard of 'im."

"Possibly." Powell handed Harry another cigarette and lit it for him. "You said he had it coming. What exactly did you mean by that?"

The landlord's eyes narrowed. "I didn't say that. I said there's *some* that thinks that."

"Fair enough, but you did mention it."

Harry shrugged. "It's no secret around these parts. Ever 'ear of a girl named Maggie Stewart?"

Powell shook his head.

"Came from an old 'Oughton Bridge family. Anyway, one summer back in the early nineties, she 'ad a fling with young Garrett—'e used to come down every year for the fishing. But after 'e had his fun with 'er, the bastard dumped 'er. Maggie never got over it and a few months later she took a rope up to 'Oughton Brook and 'anged herself. Very sad," he said, shaking his head. "Very sad."

"And you say some blame Garrett for her death?"

Harry appeared to ignore the question. "And that's not the worst of it," he continued in a husky voice. "The poor girl 'ad a bun in the oven at the time."

Powell shook his head sympathetically as he listened to

Harry's account of unrequited love, suicide, and murder in Houghton Bridge. He was struck as much by the strength of feeling the landlord's voice conveyed as by the bare facts themselves, which, while tragic, were hardly unprecedented. He glanced at his watch. "I don't wish to impose, Harry, but I'm feeling a bit peckish and I was wondering if I might get something to eat. . . ."

The landlord frowned as he considered this request. "I always say pubs is for drinking and caffs is for eating," he said, "but in your case I'll make an exception. I'll have the missus whip up a bacon butty for you. Nice bit of fat in it," he added with obvious relish.

Powell felt his stomach squirm. "On second thought, I wouldn't want to trouble your good lady. And I've just remembered I've got a few errands to run, so I'd best be off."

The landlord shrugged. "Suit yourself."

He watched as Powell walked out the door of the pub and passed by the window, then he poured himself another drink.

CHAPTER 13

Laura Miller sat tensely across the kitchen table from her husband. Through the open window came the sound of children screaming in the back garden. Sunlight flooded the room, but rather than warming her it seemed to have the effect of accentuating every imperfection— the scratched and gouged surface of the table, the mole on the back of her hand, the sharpness of her husband's features. "Everything was fine until that woman turned up," she said.

"You talk about her like that, yet you don't even know her," Miller protested.

"Not like you, not in the biblical sense." Her eyes brimmed with tears.

He shook his head in exasperation. "That was years ago. How many times do I have to tell you?"

"Then what were you doing in the fishing hut with her Tuesday morning?"

"What?"

"Are you going to sit there and deny it?"

Miller was caught off-balance. How could she possibly—? Then he remembered that Mrs. Iverson and her binoculars had been over for tea yesterday. "That interfering old bitch—"

"As always, blame anyone but yourself."

He took a deep breath. "Laura, look," he said, "you are right about one thing: I *am* concerned about Danica. She's an old friend and she's in a very vulnerable state right now. Surely you can understand that." He reached across the table and stroked her cheek. "Look at me," he said.

She brushed his hand away. "We've worked so hard and now to risk throwing it all away."

He tried to reassure her. "You and the children are everything to me, you know that."

"The fact remains," she persisted, "*someone* killed Richard Garrett and I don't want you drawn into it."

He withdrew his hand. "What exactly do you mean by that?" he asked sharply.

"Everyone knows that Danica Hughes blamed Richard Garrett for her best friend's suicide and now she's living with Brian, who's a complete bloody basket case and—"

Miller interrupted her. "So you're suggesting that Danica killed Garrett, or perhaps Brian did it, or maybe they planned it together." He shook his head in disbelief. "Christ Almighty, Laura, sometimes I wonder—" He caught himself.

She stared at him, wild-eyed. "Why you married me, you mean? Why don't you just come out and say it?"

Without another word, Miller got up and stormed out, slamming the door behind him.

PC Bailey eyed the stranger with interest. "Yes, sir, what can I do for you?"

Powell handed over his card.

The young constable's eyes widened. *Chief Superintendent Erskine Powell, Metropolitan Police Service, New Scotland Yard, Broadway, London SW1H OBG.* "Welcome to Houghton Bridge Police Station, Mr. Powell. Down for the fishing, are you? Please come in—I mean, please come into the back. I've just put the kettle on—can I offer you a cup of tea?"

Powell smiled. "Lovely."

PC Bailey fumbled with the latch on the counter door and eventually managed to swing it back. "Right through here, sir."

The police station was a converted house fronting on the High Street with a reception area and office in the front and living quarters for the constable in the rear. As Powell followed PC Bailey down the hall and into a small sitting room, he saw the unmistakable signs of bachelor living everywhere.

"You'll have to excuse the mess, sir," PC Bailey apologized, as he cleared a pile of newspapers and other domestic detritus from the coffee table. "I usually tidy up before my sarge comes," he added lamely.

Powell laughed. "If you can't be comfortable in your own home, what's the point?"

PC Bailey grinned. "Right. Make yourself comfortable, Mr. Powell, and I'll fix the tea."

Powell walked over to the window, which looked out behind the house onto a green field with horses and a line of trees beyond marking the course of the River Test. The back garden had been converted into a small car park with a garage for the police car. There were a few straggly flowers struggling along the side, obviously in need of resuscitation, and Powell immediately felt a twinge of sympathy for the young constable. He wondered how his own garden in Surbiton was faring. Then he thought about Marion, something he had tried—not entirely successfully—to avoid doing since arriving in Houghton Brook. He had promised himself that when he returned to London he would call her and they would sort it all out just like they'd always done. It was at a time like this when he missed her most, when the line between fantasy and reality was blurred. . . .

His reverie was interrupted by the return of PC Bailey.

The constable placed two mugs of tea, milk, sugar, and a plate heaped with chocolate digestives on the table. When they had settled themselves, Bailey asked about Powell's work at the Yard.

Powell began to explain about his role in the Met's Area Major Investigations Pool when PC Bailey piped up excitedly, "Isn't the AMIP much the same as the old Murder Squad?"

Powell smiled. "That's it. Of course, things aren't like they were in the old days when local police forces like

your own would call us in to help out from time to time.
You've got your own CID in Andover now."

PC Bailey, thinking about Inspector Marsh, grimaced.
"Right."

"So the activities of the AMIP are largely confined to
the Greater London Area," Powell continued. "Still, it
gets me out from behind my desk occasionally."

"It must be bloody marvelous, sir—pardon my French."

"It has its moments. But what about you, Bailey? You
must have to deal with the occasional matter of interest?"

"Nothing ever happens in Houghton Bridge, Mr.
Powell, not like London. I've only been here a little over
a year, mind you, and it's my first posting, but I suppose
I didn't expect it to be so—I don't know—so boring."

Powell nodded sympathetically. "Well, we all have to
start out somewhere. But from what I hear you've had
some excitement here recently."

"Sir?"

"The murder up at Houghton Brook this morning."

PC Bailey sighed. "Oh, that. That has nothing to do
with me, Mr. Powell. It's being handled by my sarge in
Stockbridge and a detective inspector from Andover."

"Oh, I see."

"The thing is," PC Bailey continued earnestly, "I know
I have what it takes to help out with the investigation. It's
just that, well, Inspector Marsh and I seem to have got off
on the wrong foot and—" The young constable suddenly
colored. "Forgive me, sir, I didn't mean to imply any crit-
icism of my superior." He looked devastated.

Powell smiled reassuringly. "Relax, Bailey. I'm on

holiday. Besides, if you didn't have the odd doubt about your superiors, I'd be worried about you."

PC Bailey evinced an air of relief.

Powell helped himself to another biscuit. "Now then, what do you know about this business?"

"Well, sir, I can tell you what I've managed to find out so far, which isn't much, I'm afraid." He went on to recount the facts of the case, responding to the occasional question from Powell.

Powell, for his part, was oblivious to the obvious danger sign that he had begun to think of the matter as *his* case. "Any idea at this point who might have done it?" he asked.

PC Bailey shook his head. "As a starting point, Inspector Marsh was going to interview the bloke who looks after the water meadow, as well as Mr. Street at Houghton Manor."

"Why Street?"

"The body was found on the fishing club's water. The next stretch upstream belongs to the Manor. I imagine Mr. Marsh is wondering if Mr. Street might have seen anything suspicious."

"What do you know about Simon Street?"

"Former actor, apparently. Swans about the village like he's Laurence Bloody Olivier, if you don't mind me saying so, sir."

"What about Mrs. Street?"

"Well-liked by just about everyone around here, as far as I can tell. I see her from time to time in the High Street and she seems very nice."

"Bit of an odd couple, wouldn't you say?"

"Well, sir, they do say opposites attract."

Powell frowned. "Tell me, Bailey, do you know anything about a girl named Maggie Stewart?"

PC Bailey nodded. "I've heard about her. Her brother Brian still lives in Houghton Brook. He's the bloke I mentioned who looks after the water meadow for the council—maintains the hatches in good working order, that sort of thing."

This pricked Powell's interest. "Really?" He related the Coach and Horses' landlord's account of the alleged relationship between Maggie Stewart and the murder victim, Richard Garrett.

"I hadn't heard that, Mr. Powell, but Harry should know." He looked at Powell. "Maggie Stewart was his niece."

Powell had spent the last half hour taking the measure of PC Bailey and he liked what he saw. He decided to take a chance and float a fly over the young constable, well aware that in this instance his own skin was more at risk than his quarry's. "I'll tell you what, Bailey, fishing has been slow and I'm the type who needs to keep busy. Why don't I do a little poking around? Unofficially, of course. If I stumble across anything of interest, I'll pass it along. I'm sure if you were to bring any useful information to the attention of your superiors, they would be extremely grateful."

PC Bailey was thunderstruck. He couldn't believe his ears. How often did a junior constable get an offer of assistance from a senior Scotland Yard detective and a member of the famous Murder Squad, no less? His exhilaration, however, was tempered somewhat by the thought of what Inspector Marsh would do to him if he ever caught wind of this little arrangement.

Sensing his hesitation, Powell tried to reassure him. "If anyone asks, I will deny having this conversation, so you needn't worry about getting into trouble."

"What about you, sir?"

"Not to worry," Powell lied, "I can always pull a few strings." He could well imagine the particular string, looped tightly around his own neck, that Merriman would be pulling if the assistant commissioner ever found that one of his officers had been meddling in local police affairs.

PC Bailey beamed. "You can rely on me, Mr. Powell, I won't let you down."

Suppressing a twinge of guilt, Powell leaned in closer. "Now this is what I have in mind. . . ."

CHAPTER 14

The Reverend Geoffrey Norris was deeply disturbed. It was at a time like this—a time of death and loss—that he felt most alone. Intellectually he had his faith to sustain him, but the reality of his ancient, silent church with its weed-infested churchyard affected him at a more fundamental level. If he died tomorrow, who would miss him? His elderly parishioners perhaps, clucking sympathetically over their tea for a day or two, and possibly a few others who had trusted him over the years with their doubts and fears. But they, too, would soon forget. And who would take his place, who would tend to his flock when he was gone?

He thought about the funeral he had presided over the previous morning for another member of his dwindling congregation. Winnie Greene, eighty-three years old, late of Houghton Bridge in the County of Hampshire, had grown up in the village, fallen in love, married, and played the piano. She had been widowed young and she died alone in her bed. That was about the sum of it. *Man that is born of woman hath but a short time to live, and is full of misery. He cometh up, and is cut down, like a flower,* he had intoned as they lowered her down. *Earth to earth, ashes to ashes, dust to dust . . .*

But did any of it really matter, he wondered. He had always believed that the church provided an essential service, whether one believed in the promise of eternal redemption or not. For in a universe without God, any evil, any outrage was permissible.

And then he thought about Pamela Street and the young man up at the Houghton Brook, brutally murdered in the prime of life. The memories came flooding back and it was almost more than he could bear. With trembling fingers he poured himself a glass of sherry. He was about to have another when the doorbell chimed.

"Erskine," he said. "This is a pleasant surprise. Do come in."

Powell regarded the minister's red-rimmed eyes with concern. "Geoffrey, is anything the matter?"

"Just my allergies acting up, nothing to w-worry about." He smiled. "Now then, to what do I owe this pleasure?"

"I was just passing by and thought I'd have another look round the church. I'm a bit of a history buff, you see."

The vicar appeared to perk up. "Splendid! I can give you the deluxe g-guided tour."

"If it's no trouble . . ."

"No trouble at all. In fact I'm heartened that you're

interested in St. Andrew's. But first I insist that you join me in a glass of sherry." He winked slyly. "I am given to understand that it is not socially acceptable to drink alone."

Powell smiled. "You won't have to twist my arm."

The vicar ushered him into the sitting room, made sure he was comfortable, then handed him a glass. "Have you been enjoying your stay in Houghton Bridge?" he asked.

"Very much. I've done a bit of fishing and seen some of the sights—and I must say, St. Andrew's is one of the highlights. And I've been delving a bit into the local history."

"Ah, then you must have been up to the Iron Age hillfort at Danebury?"

Powell looked at him. "I'm more interested in recent history, actually."

"R-really?"

"I imagine you've heard about the incident up at the weir this morning. . . ."

The vicar shook his head sadly. "Tragic business, simply tragic."

"Did you know the young man?"

"Not personally, but I knew of him. . . ." The vicar hesitated. "Forgive me if this sounds impertinent, but m-may I ask why you are interested? Have the local police asked you to assist them with their inquiries?"

Powell smiled easily. "Nothing as formal as all that. Let's just say that I'm interested in helping out if I can."

The vicar seemed satisfied with this explanation, even slightly relieved. "If there is anything I can do, Erskine, please don't hesitate to ask."

"Perhaps you can start by telling me what you know about Richard Garrett."

The vicar seemed to consider this for a moment. "I didn't know him personally," he began. "His father is a m-member of the fishing club—you know all about the Mayfly Club, I presume. . . ."

Powell nodded.

"Young Richard used to come down for the fishing every season, but hadn't done so for a number of years. As a matter of fact, I believe this is the first time he'd been back since—I should say in seven or eight years."

"Do you have any idea why he stayed away for all that time?"

"I-I believe there was an affair of the heart involved," the vicar replied.

"Can you elaborate?"

The vicar hesitated. "You are leading me onto shaky ground, I'm afraid. I must be careful not to betray a confidence. You can no doubt imagine that a minister is occasionally told something by a parishioner that isn't intended for public consumption." He smiled. "It's a b-bit like solicitor-client privilege, I suppose."

"I understand completely."

"I can tell you this, however: Richard Garrett was basically an honorable man who has been much maligned by certain people in this village, not necessarily out of malice, but out of ignorance, I fear."

"I understand that the affair of the heart you mentioned involved a girl named Maggie Stewart."

The vicar sighed. "You've heard all about it, then."

"I've heard that Garrett got Ms. Stewart pregnant, then ended the affair, which led eventually to her suicide. However, you seem to paint quite a different picture."

"I suppose it all depends on where you g-get your information," the vicar replied with uncharacteristic curtness. "Maggie Stewart would be the last person to—" He checked himself. "In any case, I've given you my opinion of young Garrett."

Powell's reply was cut short by the doorbell ringing.

The vicar rose to his feet. "Please excuse me."

There was the sound of muffled voices and when the vicar returned a few moments later, he seemed preoccupied. "I'm terribly sorry, Erskine, but one of my p-parishioners wishes to speak with me. Perhaps I could show you around St. Andrew's another time."

"Of course, Geoffrey."

As Powell followed his host down the hall, he glanced through a doorway on the left and saw a well-dressed, middle-aged woman watching him. He smiled, but she appeared to look right through him.

Sir Robert Alderson sighed. He had intended on returning to London for the weekend, but had changed his plans so that he could be in Houghton Bridge to comfort his old friend Bernard Garrett when he arrived tomorrow. But now that was all up in the air. He had just got off the telephone with one of Bernard's associates, who informed him that Bernard, who had a weak heart, had taken a turn and been ordered by his doctor not to travel.

As Sir Robert looked out over the village from his

window on the second floor of the Mayfly Inn, he wondered a trifle wistfully if it might all be just a bad dream. In the fading sunlight, the tidy row of shops and houses along the High Street gleamed like jewels amidst a green baize fold of hills. It seemed almost inconceivable that Houghton Bridge was beset by another tragedy. More to the point, he found it difficult to accept that the Mayfly Club, whose image he had carefully tended and nurtured over the years, was implicated once again in something decidedly unsavory.

He would have been the first to admit that it was the reputation of the Mayfly Club that preoccupied him at the moment, rather than the fate of Richard Garrett. It was not that he was callous or uncaring; he was simply being realistic. He could do nothing for young Garrett, and his clear duty now was to ensure that the venerable institution with which he was entrusted did not founder on his watch.

In a very real sense the continuing existence of the Mayfly Club depended on the goodwill of the local population. Sir Robert, by virtue of his biological training, viewed the arrangement as something akin to symbiosis, the process whereby two organisms coexist in an intimate relationship to their mutual benefit.

There was no disputing the fact that the River Test's fame as a trout fishery was due in no small part to the existence of the Mayfly Club, whose membership had included such luminaries as the painter J. M. W. Turner and more than one prime minister. The club tended to keep a relatively low profile these days, with members jealously guarding their anonymity. However, it was this cachet that continued to attract anglers from all over the world to Houghton Bridge. These visitors spent considerable sums of money in the village and surrounding area whilst fishing on their rented beats.

For its part, in addition to the benefits it derived from various business interests in the area, the Mayfly Club enjoyed a position of influence with the local council. Over the years the club had been instrumental in averting a number of development schemes that would have had a disastrous impact on the river and, by extension, on the traditional way of life in Houghton Bridge and the surrounding countryside.

It was with a clear conscience, therefore, that Sir Robert Alderson sat in his room that evening considering how to best turn the day's unfortunate events to the Mayfly Club's advantage. An egalitarian by nature, Sir Robert strenuously resisted all arguments that the Mayfly Club was a bastion of elitism and privilege that epitomized everything that was wrong with British society. These days, most of the club's members were self-made men who had achieved their station in life by virtue of hard work rather than by the class to which they were born. Still, there was no denying the club's exclusivity, which, considering the delicacy of the matter at hand, presented certain obvious difficulties.

His brow furrowed as he thought about the suicide of that girl seven years ago and her association with young Garrett. Being a man of science, he did not believe in coincidences. Neither was he superstitious. Yet he could not dispel the unsettling feeling that the final act of this tragedy had yet to be played out.

The following morning, Brian Stewart read Danica's note with numb disbelief. He felt like he was dreaming, unable to focus around the edges of his thoughts. Her words were clear enough: *Brian, Returning to London. Please don't try to contact me. Good luck. Love, Dani.* But what could it mean? Her bed not slept in, the torn scrap of paper on the kitchen table when he got up, the cold silent house reeking of stale beer. His first reaction had been to search the cottage with manic intensity, calling her name, looking in every room and closet, then outside in the greenhouse, and finally—almost as an afterthought—the garage. Her car was gone, so he tried her mobile phone but there was no answer.

For the next hour he sat at the table, paralyzed, staring at the note, mouthing her words over and over like a mantra, as if by doing so he might transcend the awful reality of it. A hundred thoughts and images were jumbled together in his head. He suppressed a wave of panic. Why had she left him? Who would help him now? Once again he read her note aloud—

There was a sharp rapping on the door. He leaped to his feet and ran to open it. "Dani!" he cried out as he fumbled with the latch.

A uniformed police officer stood on the step. "Brian Stewart? We'd like a word with you, sir."

CHAPTER 15

It struck Powell that Jim Hardy seemed strangely subdued as he moved about the sunlit dining room serving breakfast to his guests. Powell was beginning to feel a bit guilty. The guesthouse was fully booked, and despite the fact that he had the rather dour Mrs. Fielding to help with the meals and housekeeping, Jim gave the distinct impression that he had his hands full. Powell had originally intended to leave on Sunday, but now he was torn. On the one hand, he knew he could occupy himself for several days longer assisting Constable Bailey with his inquiries, as he euphemistically liked to think of it. On the other hand, he was concerned about imposing any longer on his host. And, most pressing of all, he reminded himself, he needed some time at home to sort things out with Marion before he returned to work.

His reverie was interrupted by the arrival at his table of Jim Hardy with a dismal-looking couple in tow. His host looked apologetic. "We're a bit full this morning,

Erskine. I hope you don't mind if Mr. and Mrs. Dorking join you for breakfast."

Powell felt a cold hand grip his heart as he thought about this pair watching him consume his full English. He smiled. "Of course not," he lied.

It turned out that Mr. Dorking, a small, pinched man with a nasal voice, was a greengrocer from Lyme Regis; Mrs. Dorking, for her part, was the spitting image of Margaret Thatcher.

"One would have thought," Mrs. Dorking pronounced ponderously, "that for the prices they charge, one would have been given a table of one's own."

"Oh, I don't know, Mrs. Dorking. I always feel that one of the great things about traveling is the opportunity to share experiences with fellow travelers. My name is Powell, by the way. Erskine Powell."

"Odd sort of name," Mrs. Dorking concluded.

"What brings you to Houghton Bridge, Mr. Powell?" her husband piped up bravely.

"I'm here for the fishing, Mr. Dorking. Are you an angler, by any chance?"

Mr. Dorking shook his head sadly.

"Useless sort of sport," Mrs. Dorking opined.

"And what brings you and your husband to the Test Valley?"

She smiled a flinty smile. "We're in the market for a place in the country, a weekend getaway until Mr. Dorking retires. It must have all mod cons, of course, but one longs for the peace and tranquillity of the countryside. Don't you agree, Mr. Powell?"

Powell's heart went out to Mr. Dorking. A weekend getaway with Mrs. Dorking didn't bear thinking about, let alone a lingering retirement in an isolated country house. "Appearances are not always what they seem, Mrs. Dorking. *'It is my belief, . . . founded upon my experience, that the lowest and vilest alleys of London do not present a more dreadful record of sin than does the smiling and beautiful countryside.'* "

She eyed him suspiciously. "What?"

"Sherlock Holmes, Mrs. Dorking."

Mr. Dorking suddenly brightened. "You must be referring to that murder!"

His wife cast him a withering glance. "That's quite enough, Stanley, we don't wish to spoil Mr. Powell's breakfast."

"Not at all, Mrs. Dorking. I would be most interested to hear what your husband has to say."

Mr. Dorking swallowed nervously. "Yes, well, I read all about it in the local paper this morning. You could say that murder is a hobby of mine"—he suddenly looked mortified and went on quickly to explain—"that is to say I make it a habit to follow such cases closely."

Powell smiled. "Well, Stanley—may I call you Stanley?—it seems we have much in common."

Mr. Dorking, taking this as a sign of encouragement, forged ahead, his voice becoming increasingly animated as he warmed to his subject. "What drives an ordinary person to commit the ultimate crime, Mr. Powell? That's the fascinating thing about murder, if you want my opinion, not the sordid details of the knife penetrating living flesh, the recoil of the bullet, or the gushing of blood."

There was considerable clucking from Mrs. Dorking at this point, arising perhaps from the realization that her husband had a vivid and hitherto unsuspected inner life.

"The details of each case can vary in a hundred different ways," he continued, "but basic human motivations never change. It always comes down to revenge, fear, lust, hatred, or greed. You can keep your DNA and your boffins in white lab coats," he concluded smugly. "Look to human nature and you won't go far wrong."

Mr. Dorking clearly had given the subject considerable thought, and Powell made a determined effort not to look at Mrs. Dorking for fear of putting ideas into his head. He drained his coffee cup with a flourish. "This is absolutely fascinating and I'd love to continue our discussion, but I'm afraid the trout are calling and I must run. Cheerio." And with that he fled the dining room.

"Very rude," Mrs. Dorking sniffed.

When Powell stepped outside into the morning sunshine, fishing was the farthest thing from his mind. Oddly enough, the greengrocer's facile analysis had got him thinking.

On his way to the Test Bridge, Powell bumped into PC Bailey doing his rounds and learned that Brian Stewart, Maggie Stewart's brother, had been detained for questioning.

"What do you make of it?" Powell asked.

"Brian's a strange sort of bird—bit of a loner." PC Bailey rubbed his chin thoughtfully. "He strikes me as being quite harmless, although I've heard it said that he's not been the same since his sister died."

"Any idea why he was brought in?"

"Well, sir, it turns out he had an altercation with Garrett in the High Street the day before the murder."

"What kind of altercation?"

"I haven't got all the details, but apparently Stewart was overheard threatening Garrett."

"Really? Would you say that was in character?"

PC Bailey shrugged. "Like I said, sir, he seems like a quiet bloke."

"Well, Bailey, see what else you can find out. I'll pop in to see you later."

PC Bailey smiled. "Beautiful morning for a walk, sir."

Powell grunted, then continued along the High Street.

The river path took off from the road just before the old stone bridge that crossed the River Test at the edge of the village. It dipped steeply down to the meadow and then followed closely beside the river, curving gradually to the right toward a line of trees in the distance that marked the course of the Houghton Brook. About a hundred yards along there was someone fishing. As Powell walked along the path, amidst the sound of twittering birds, he noticed a few mayflies fluttering overhead. As he got closer he saw that the fisherman was in fact a young woman in thigh-length waders, and he decided to stop and watch her fish. She was standing about fifty feet upstream and hadn't noticed him, being intent on persuading a particularly stubborn trout to take her fly. Powell's curiosity was piqued.

He sat down on a wooden bench fortuitously provided for the purpose and called out to her. She turned, a look of surprise on her face.

"I hope you don't mind if I watch," Powell said, smiling.

"Not at all," she replied coolly, sizing him up. "You can even take notes if you like."

"I might just do that. By the way, I'd put on a mayfly if I were you. The hatch should be starting soon."

"Would you now? If you'd been paying attention to the water you'd have noticed that it started five minutes ago."

She began to false cast and with an expert flick of her wrist laid her line gently on the water. A second later there was a loud splash and her rod bent under the strain of a sizable fish. Powell strolled over to monitor the proceedings.

"Let me know if you need a hand landing it," he offered.

"I don't think that will be necessary," she rejoined. A few minutes later she slid the fish, a wild brown trout weighing about a pound and a half, into the weedy shallows. She knelt down and freed the hook from the corner of its mouth, then cradled the fish gently in her hands and returned it to the water. With a splash of its tail it was gone.

She stood up and looked at Powell, brushing her hair from her eyes with the back of her wrist. "Would you care to have a go?" she said.

"Thanks all the same, Ms. . . . ?"

"Walker. Jemma Walker."

"My name's Powell." He held out his hand.

She smiled. "I'm all slimy."

He laughed. "Right."

"Are you sure you don't want to give it a try?"

"It's quite all right. As a matter-of-fact, I've been doing quite well myself on the Houghton Brook. With an Iron Blue Dun."

"A what?"

"Er, it's an older pattern."

"I see. Tell me, Powell, do you make a habit of spying on women when they're fishing?"

"Only when they belong to the famous Mayfly Fishing Club."

"I'll ignore that. But perhaps I can interest you in a cup of tea, as I've no doubt your misguided offer of assistance was well intentioned. I feel it's the least I can do."

"Thank you, Ms. Walker. I think."

She smiled again. "It's Jemma." She slipped off her fishing vest, rummaged about in the back pocket for a moment, and produced a thermos flask and two plastic cups. She gestured toward the bench.

"You were wrong about one thing," she said.

"Oh yes?"

"I'm not a member of the Mayfly Club."

"A poacher, then?"

She laughed. "Not exactly."

"I must say this is highly suspicious . . ."

"I could ask what business it is of yours."

"It may just seem like a bit of poaching to you, Jemma, but this sort of thing if left unchecked eventually leads to general anarchy and depravity."

"I'm not too keen on the anarchy bit," she replied archly. "But if you must know, I've been nominated for membership in the club and I happen to be fishing as a guest."

"From what little I know of it, I would have thought that the Mayfly Club was one of the last bastions of the old boys' network," Powell observed mischievously.

She regarded him with amusement. "I can outfish most of them, you know."

It occurred to Powell, as he chatted beside the river with Jemma Walker, that he felt completely at ease in her company. It was as if he'd known her for ages. She was also extremely attractive. When he'd finished his tea, he set off once again on his walk, but not before he'd arranged to meet her for a drink that evening—to learn more about the Mayfly Club, he reminded himself.

CHAPTER 16

After a fruitless attempt to penetrate the defenses of the crime scene on the Houghton Brook, which consisted of festoons of yellow police ribbon and a large humorless constable, Powell returned to Mill House to snatch an hour's fishing before lunch. But by the time he had retrieved his tackle and arrived at his beat, the mayfly hatch had subsided and all he could manage was a couple of tiddlers on the Iron Blue Dun. He didn't suppose that Jemma Walker would be very impressed.

He grabbed a sandwich at the guesthouse and then set off to see his old mate Harry at the Coach and Horses. When he walked in the door, all of the usual suspects were in attendance. He received a frosty reception.

"What do you recommend today, Harry?" he asked, surveying the row of taps.

"You can read," the landlord muttered.

"Yes, well, I'll have a half of Gale's, please."

The landlord complied in sullen silence.

"Lovely day."

"Could be better." He began to polish the bar with a grubby rag.

"Any news on your murder?"

Harry stopped what he was doing and looked up. "You ask a lot of questions. Just like a flipping copper."

Powell was somewhat taken aback, but soldiered on. "I understand that the police have a suspect in mind."

The landlord walked slowly over and leaned perilously close, glaring at Powell with bloodshot intensity. "I wouldn't know about that," he hissed. "Now finish your drink and get the fuck out." He tossed his rag into the sink and disappeared into the back room.

Powell felt all eyes on him as he gulped down his beer. After a decent interval, he left the pub and paid a visit to the police station.

PC Bailey looked alarmed. "I have no idea how he could have found out about you, Mr. Powell. I hope you don't think that—"

Powell frowned. He couldn't help wondering about Jim Hardy. "Of course not, Bailey, but the word getting out does complicate matters. Old Harry was extremely forth-right when he thought I was just your garden-variety busybody."

"Perhaps he just doesn't like policemen, sir."

"Who does, Bailey?"

The young constable sighed. "Right."

"The thing that struck me about Harry—what's his last name?"

"Watts, sir."

"You mentioned before that Maggie Stewart was his niece."

PC Bailey nodded. "His sister was Maggie's mother."

"Was?"

"She died in a car crash several years ago."

"Before or after her daughter's suicide?"

"A few months after."

"What about her father?"

"Moved away when his wife died. I think he's living up north, Lancashire or somewhere like that."

"For someone who hasn't been here very long, you seem to know quite a bit about the local history."

PC Bailey grinned. "Well, sir, I've been doing a bit of digging on my own."

"Initiative is a great thing, Bailey. Keep it up. In the meantime, I'm going to have to watch myself. The last thing either of us needs is for your brass to find out about my interest in the case."

PC Bailey nodded.

"Any word on the brother?"

"Apparently he's clammed up. Won't say exactly where he was at the time in question, or whether he saw anything, although it seems that he was mucking about the water meadow yesterday morning."

Powell grunted. "What's next?"

"Well, we've got until tomorrow morning to make up our minds, then we can either nick him or go before a magistrate to ask for another twenty-four hours."

"I *am* aware of the legal process, Bailey."

PC Bailey reddened. "Sorry, sir."

"I was wondering if your colleagues are pursuing any other leads."

"Funny you should mention it, sir. I just got off the phone with one of my mates in Stockbridge when you arrived and it seems that Brian Stewart has had a friend staying with him for the past couple of weeks—a young woman named Danica Hughes. The funny thing is, Mr. Powell, she seems to have suddenly dropped out of sight."

This caught Powell's attention. "Do you know anything about her?"

"She was born and raised in Houghton Bridge. Her father was the former riverkeeper for the fishing club. And that's not the most interesting thing about her. . . ." He paused dramatically.

Powell sighed. "Yes, Bailey?"

"Well, sir, it seems that Danica Hughes was Maggie Stewart's best friend."

"Hmm. You say she'd been back for a couple of weeks. Would you know her if you saw her?"

PC Bailey shook his head. "There are so many visitors in the village this time of year."

Powell frowned. "I wonder what Brian Stewart has to say about her disappearance?"

PC Bailey shrugged.

Powell puzzled over something. "I keep thinking about Harry Watts's reaction this afternoon," he said. "It was as if he held me personally responsible for the police's interest in his nephew."

"Perhaps it's beginning to hit a little too close to home," PC Bailey replied.

Powell looked at him, but said nothing.

The office phone jangled discordantly for several seconds before Jim Hardy made a decision to answer it. He cursed silently. It irritated him to no end that Mrs. Fielding hadn't bothered to pick up the extension in the kitchen, where she was preparing the evening meal. He had been on his way out to do some shopping when he discovered at the last moment that he had misplaced his list. The phone had interrupted him as he was rummaging amongst his papers. As he stood there trying to ignore the persistent double ring, he was seized with the realization that the guesthouse was quickly becoming a burden instead of the joy it had once been.

He took a deep breath and picked up the receiver. "Mill House."

His expression tightened. "Yes, I do recall our conversation—I told you then that I was open to discussing the rent."

The voice droned in his ear.

"Look, if you don't mind, I'd prefer to speak to Mrs. Street about this. . . ."

He listened numbly for several seconds more. "Simply a business decision . . . I see." He thought about mounting a counterargument, but the voice on the other end was implacable and he was damned if he was going to crawl.

He made a concerted effort to remain calm, speaking with exaggerated precision. "I've heard you out, Street, now you listen to me. I know all about your exploits, and I'm sure Mrs. Street would be interested in hearing what I have to say." He went on to make himself perfectly clear.

There was a burst of noise on the other end of the line.

"That's such an unpleasant word, but you can call it whatever you like. . . . Well, we'll just have to see about that—"

Click.

Hardy sat slumped at his desk for several minutes, considering the implications of the telephone call. He supposed he should have seen it coming, but it didn't really matter because he knew he hadn't a leg to stand on. When you came right down to it, he was no more than a tenant whose business operated at the pleasure of the landlord. The stark reality was that everything he had worked for all these years now hung in the balance, and there was absolutely nothing he could do about it. He could only hope that his pathetic bluff would have some effect.

CHAPTER 17

"Tell me, how did a nice girl like you end up in a place like this?" Powell asked, raising his voice above the Friday night din at the Mayfly Inn.

Jemma Walker smiled. "That's original. In a hangout for fly fishermen, you mean?"

"If you like."

"It all started when I was four or five. I was a bit of a tomboy, and my dad used to take me fishing with him every Sunday on our local river. Anyway, it wasn't long before I was, um, hooked. It was coarse fishing then, but I eventually graduated to trout and salmon. The problem was, I could never find anyone who wanted to go fishing with me. I had the occasional male friend who made a halfhearted effort, but more on the pretext of landing *me,* I suspect."

Powell could well imagine.

She started to laugh. "I remember once I persuaded a

girlfriend to join me for a weekend on the Wiltshire Avon. She had somehow got the idea that fly fishing was sexy, but soon found that sloshing around in crotch-high rubber boots didn't exactly make her feel like a sex goddess."

Powell chuckled. "Hold that thought." He drained his glass. "May I get you another?"

"That would be nice."

He jostled his way to the bar and returned a short time later with another pint and a glass of Chablis.

"You were telling me about your expedition to the wilds of Wiltshire," he prompted.

She sipped her wine. "Right. We were staying in this big country house belonging to a business associate of mine. It was a few centuries old, situated right on the river with long rows of lime trees and an artificial lake right out of Capability Brown. Anyway, the first afternoon, Angela—that's my friend—fell in the river and nearly caught her death. She spent the rest of the weekend trying to get warm. First she piled on the sweaters, which marked her forever as a lily-livered townie. Then she would hog the fire after dinner before ensconcing herself in the tub for the remainder of the evening. I can tell you that the sound of good hot water gushing onto white enamel was extremely painful for our host. To top it all off, neither of us caught a thing all weekend. Needless to say I haven't been invited back."

Powell laughed. "It takes a special sort of woman to make a good fisherman."

"Careful," Jemma warned.

"Let me rephrase that—" he pondered for a moment "— it is important, I think, to choose one's fishing companions wisely."

"That's better. In my case, it wasn't until I got to university that I finally met a kindred spirit, someone who was as mad about fishing as I was."

"Really."

"Sir Robert Alderson, one of my professors at Cambridge."

Powell nearly choked on his beer. "Good God! It's like old home week."

He went on to explain that he was a Cantabrigian himself, as was Jim Hardy at Mill House, where he was staying.

She shook her head in amazement. "I knew there was something peculiar about you when we first met."

"You mean you felt a certain affinity with a kindred spirit."

She laughed. "Not exactly."

Powell leaned back in his chair. He was dying for a cigarette, but resisted the urge. "Tell me more about Sir Robert."

"Where to start? Let's see . . . Bob is a world-renowned surgeon, not to mention the best fly fisherman I've ever met; he was instrumental in my decision to start my own biotech company; he's currently the secretary of the Mayfly Club; and, um, he's the person who put my name forward for membership. How's that for starters?"

"Very impressive."

She regarded her empty glass speculatively. "My round, I think."

When she returned with their drinks, Powell pressed her about the Mayfly Club.

"I suppose you're wondering why I'd want to belong to a club made up largely of elderly gentlemen," she said.

"The thought had crossed my mind."

"It's quite simple, really. My two passions in life are my firm and fly fishing. The Mayfly Club offers some of the best dry fly fishing in the world, and my company has prospered to the point where I can now afford it. My only qualification for membership is I'm a damn good fisherman. And the fact that I've been nominated by the club secretary doesn't hurt, either."

Powell found her candor refreshing. "How does one actually become a member?" he asked.

"When a vacancy occurs—and basically someone has to drop dead for that to happen—three names are put forward for consideration by the other members. A secret election is held—sort of a variation on the old blackball routine—and a winner is declared. It's all very civilized, I can assure you."

"Tell me about your rivals?"

"Well, there's Stephen Solomon—he's sitting just over there in the corner, as a matter of fact. Stephen's the one with the gray hair. The man he's with is the club's riverkeeper, John Miller."

"What's Mr. Solomon's claim to fame?"

"He's a big name in the City, apparently." She hesitated.

"The third candidate was Richard Garrett, and you know what happened to him."

"I thought you said it was all very civilized," Powell said blandly.

Her eyes flashed angrily. "I don't find that the least bit funny."

"Sorry."

"I'm as shocked as anyone," she said. "It's inconceivable to me that anyone could do such a thing to another human being."

Powell sighed. "If only it were so."

She studied his face for a moment. "I forgot that you have to deal with this sort of thing all the time. It must get to you after a while."

"One adapts," he replied casually. By smoking and drinking too much and letting one's marriage go to hell, he thought. "What do you think your chances are?"

"By any reckoning, I'd have to be considered a long shot. The thought of a woman in the Mayfly Club is probably a nonstarter for most of the members. Bob has been wonderful, of course, but I expect he is fighting an uphill battle."

"That leaves Stephen Solomon then."

She shrugged lightly. "I don't mind, really. He probably feels he has more to gain than I do."

Powell wondered exactly what she meant by that. He supposed that apart from the obvious status value of belonging to a clique with the pedigree of the Mayfly Club, there could be financial benefits as well. Inviting an important client for a day's fishing on the Test took the practice of wining and dining to a whole new level. "Getting back to Richard Garrett," he said, "what can you tell me about him?"

She looked at him quizzically. "Why all the questions? Is this some sort of busman's holiday for you?"

"Just making conversation, that's all."

"I see," she said in a skeptical tone. "What exactly do you want to know?"

"How well did you know him?"

"I just met him for the first time a few days ago."

"What were your impressions?"

She shrugged. "I don't know . . . he seemed nice enough, good-looking, outgoing."

"Do you know anything about his background?"

"Well, I know he was a barrister in his father's firm and quite good at it, by all accounts. I met Bernard—that's his father—on a previous visit here."

"What about his personal life?"

"What do you mean?"

"I understand he was involved in some sort of scandal with a local girl several years ago."

She sighed. "Oh, that. Look, Powell, I try not to pass judgment on other people's personal lives."

"I wasn't asking you to. I was simply asking you to corroborate what I've already heard."

"Which is?"

"That he had an affair with a young woman named Maggie Stewart and then broke it off after he got her pregnant. She committed suicide a few months later."

She looked at him with an odd expression on her face. "I suppose that's one possible interpretation of events."

"I'd be interested in hearing another version," he said pointedly.

She sighed. "I'm finding this all a bit depressing. Do you mind if we change the subject?"

"No, of course not." He smiled. "You'll have to forgive me; I seem to have slipped unconsciously into my Spanish Inquisition mode."

She returned his smile. "That's okay."

Neither of them spoke for a few moments.

Powell cleared his throat. "Er, Jemma, do you have any plans for tonight—for dinner, I mean?"

There was a hint of amusement in her eyes. "That all depends. What did you have in mind?"

"Well, to be honest, I'm craving a curry. Unfortunately the nearest Indian restaurant is in Chilbolton."

She smiled. "I quite like a good curry myself after a night of boozing, but neither of us is in any condition to drive. Any other suggestions?"

"How about the Peking Duck?"

She burst out laughing. "The peeking what?"

He fixed her with a patient look. "I was referring to the Chinese restaurant in the village, which I understand is an estimable establishment in every respect."

She affected a serious demeanor. "Right." She cleared her throat. "First I'd like to propose a toast." She raised her glass and gestured for Powell to do the same. "To the Iron Blue Dun—long may she reign."

Powell grinned. "The Iron Blue Dun," he repeated as they clinked glasses. He looked at Jemma Walker appraisingly. "Exactly what line of work are you in, anyway?"

She leaned forward, placed her elbows on the table, and rested her head in her hands. She looked into his eyes and smiled. "I mend broken hearts," she said.

CHAPTER 18

The next day Powell felt slightly the worse for the previous evening's festivities. Jemma Walker had regaled him into the wee small hours with stories of salmon fishing in Iceland, fishing for bonefish in Cuba, steelhead fishing in British Columbia, and a few other places besides which he couldn't remember at the moment. He vaguely recalled borrowing a torch and making his way unsteadily back to Mill House around midnight. He had got up rather late, nearly missing breakfast, and eventually emerged into the bright sunlight of another promising Hampshire morning.

He had drawn the bottom beat just above the Manor water for the morning and as chance would have it Jemma was fishing on the club water just downstream. They had agreed to meet for lunch on her beat and it was there that he now headed, having had a relatively successful morning, all things considered, with three good trout caught and released. As he walked along the river path beside the

Houghton Brook, past the small white sign with red lettering that indicated the boundary between the guest-house water and the stretch reserved for the Manor, he was preoccupied with the murder of Richard Garrett.

Here was a young man with a promising future ahead of him, who had met a violent end amidst the most pastoral of surroundings. And it had quickly become evident that those who had known him divided into two distinct camps. But as Powell thought about it, it occurred to him that his conflicting impressions of Garrett were based solely on what he had heard from Harry Watts, the proprietor of the Coach and Horses, and from the Reverend Norris. It was clear that Watts blamed Garrett for his niece's suicide; in the vicar's case, Powell concluded that he must know something that had led him to believe that Garrett was basically a decent sort. Powell made a mental note to pay another visit to St. Andrew's.

Up ahead on the opposite bank a fisherman was flogging the water. His movements were jerky and awkward, suggesting a sort of pent-up fury. When he got a little closer, Powell recognized Simon Street. The lord of the Manor was kitted up in fine form in a jacket and tie with a canvas fishing bag slung over his shoulder. Beside him, flopping desperately on the grass, was a small trout.

Powell stopped to watch him.

Street noticed him and stopped suddenly in mid-cast. His line landed in a tangled mess on the water. "What are you staring at?" he demanded.

"Shouldn't you do something about that fish?" Powell said. "It's suffering, you know."

"Sod the fish!" Street barked. "And you can mind your own fucking business. This is private water, so bugger off."

Powell smiled benignly. "The path, however, is a public right-of-way. I don't wish to interfere with your sport, but you really should attend to that trout. It's the sort of thing that gives all fishermen a bad name."

Amidst another barrage of expletives from Street, Powell continued on his way. He crossed the main road just before the bridge and carried on along the path until he came to the location where Richard Garrett's body had been found.

He was relieved to find that there was no policeman in attendance; it seemed that the locals had completed their scene-of-crime investigations. He decided to take the opportunity to have a look around. He crossed over the carrier stream on a wooden plank and walked through the trees to the hatchway. The iron sluice gate was partially raised and a good flow of water rushed into the ditch. He knew that the carrier flowed through the water meadow and crossed the High Street in the village before eventually flowing back into the Test. The concrete face of the weir was a conspicuously lighter color than the sides, suggesting that it had recently been scrubbed clean.

He leaned his rod against a tree and stepped up onto the top of the concrete wall. He examined the ratchet mechanism; everything looked in order. He assumed that the iron bar used to turn it had been taken as evidence. According to PC Bailey, someone had bashed Garrett on the head with the bar, then placed his head on the top of the weir, as one might position someone in a guillotine, before lowering the heavy gate onto his neck. Powell frowned. It all seemed too elaborate, as if someone were trying to make a point—albeit a none-too-subtle one. But why?

He turned to look at the upstream face of the weir. The water, which was backed up by the main weir across the Houghton Brook just downstream, appeared to be at least two feet deep, so whoever had dragged Garrett into the sluiceway would have got wet unless he was wearing waders.

The carrier took off on the outside of a long sweeping bend in the stream. Looking upstream, he could just see where the river path emerged from behind the trees and turned right around the corner toward the bridge, which was out of sight. Downstream to his left, the stream curved gently to the right for about a hundred yards and then sharply left. There was no sign of Jemma, and he assumed she must be fishing just around the corner. It struck him that this was the one section of the Houghton Brook that was relatively secluded and not readily visible from the path. He glanced at his watch and decided he had better shift.

He was just about to climb off the wall when he was startled by a loud splash. A good trout had jumped not ten feet away, the concentric rings of its rise spreading over the smooth surface of the water like so many karmic vibrations.

*　*　*

Jemma Walker smiled. "I was beginning to think you'd forgotten." She was sitting on a plaid blanket beside the stream with the picnic things already spread out.

"I wasn't that far gone last night, I hope."

"No comment. But I *have* brought iced tea instead of wine."

Powell grimaced. "Very wise." He sat down beside her. "How's fishing?"

"Slow. To be honest, I haven't risen a thing all morning. You?"

"Oh, I've had one or two," he replied nonchalantly. "On the Iron Blue Dun, of course."

She laughed. "You're insufferable, did you know that?"

"That's what my wife tells me."

She looked at him. "On balance, I'd say she's a very lucky woman."

"Yes, well, she might have something to say about that."

There was a slightly awkward interval as Jemma unwrapped the sandwiches.

Anxious to change the subject, Powell mentioned his encounter with Simon Street.

"Oh, that one! He's such a prat."

"You know him?"

"Only from the occasional, unpleasant encounter on the water. Houghton Manor actually owns all of the fishing on the Houghton Brook—"

"I'd assumed that the club owned its water outright," Powell interjected.

"Only on the Test proper. The club has a long-term

lease on the Houghton Brook downstream of the main road bridge that was negotiated many years ago with Colonel Waddington. The fishing rights are undoubtedly worth a lot more now and it's painfully obvious that Street resents the fact. Anyway, he is a thoroughly unpleasant character and I try to stay well clear of him."

Powell nodded. "What do you know about Mrs. Street?"

"Only what I've heard from Bob. I get the impression he thinks highly of her."

Something suddenly occurred to Powell. "You wouldn't happen to know anything about an alleged poaching incident involving Street, would you?"

"It's funny you should mention that. Bob and I were just talking about it the other night. It's hard to believe, isn't it?"

"I'm dying to hear your version of the story."

She looked at him. "Isn't this where you usually do your naked swinging lightbulb routine?"

"Naked swinging what?"

She smiled indulgently. "It happened about eight years ago, I think. At that time there was a particular trout residing in the Houghton Bridge in the stretch of water between the bridge and the main weir. It had lived there for a number of years, eluding all attempts to catch it, growing very large and wily. It soon became the stuff of legend. It was often seen rising, and Bob claims he hooked it once or twice, as did a few of the other members, but it always managed to break off by virtue of sheer brute strength. Anyway, one morning Garrett was fishing above the weir and—"

"Richard or his father?"

"Richard."

He gestured absently for her to continue.

"According to Bob, Richard hooked and lost the fish in the pool below the bridge. Simon Street was fishing just above the bridge at the time and apparently witnessed the whole thing. When Richard went back the next morning, there was no sign of the trout despite there being a good hatch of mayfly. The giant trout was never seen again, and the consensus seems to be that Street poached it."

Powell looked doubtful. "The evidence is a bit circumstantial, don't you think?"

"I suppose."

Powell persisted. "What's the theory as to how Street might have pulled it off? Fishing on someone else's water in full view of a public footpath would be a bit risky, I should think."

"Bob suspects that Street waited until evening, then he let his fly drift down into the club water from up above the bridge."

"You mean he caught the trout on a downstream nymph?"

She grinned. "Disgusting, isn't it? But it does make sense. By fishing down like that, the fish would see the fly before it saw the line, and you could get away with a leader strong enough to haul it quickly upstream once you'd hooked it."

"You seem to know quite a lot about the technique," Powell remarked.

"I'll ignore that."

"Where exactly is the fishing boundary located in relation to the bridge?"

"The upstream side of the bridge marks the downstream end of the Manor fishing."

"And under the bridge itself?"

"Club water."

Powell nodded. "Was anything done about it at the time?"

She shook her head. "Apparently not. As you say, there was no hard proof, and accusing somebody of poaching is a fairly serious matter. I gather Bob was concerned about Mrs. Street's reputation as well. But knowing now what Street is like, I wouldn't put it past him."

Powell nodded. "Still, you have to wonder why he'd pull a stunt like that."

"Beats me."

Powell regarded her speculatively. "You've just given me an idea," he said. "Why don't you and I have a little competition?"

"What did you have in mind?" she asked warily.

"The Mayfly versus the Iron Blue Dun. Winner takes all."

"And the stakes?"

"The one with the smallest catch, based on the total length of all fish caught, has to act as the other's gilly for a day."

"You mean you'd carry my bag, serve me lunch, and, um, cater to my every whim . . . for an entire day?"

"Don't be cheeky; you haven't won yet."

She had a gleam in her eye. "You're on, mate."

CHAPTER 19

Powell sat with PC Bailey in Ye Olde Tea Shoppe attempting to dissect a scone that had the consistency of a hockey puck. It was about four o'clock, and there were several other customers in attendance. The two policemen sat in a back corner where they wouldn't be overheard.

"Did Brian Stewart provide any useful information before your chaps had to let him go?" Powell asked.

"Yes and no, sir. He claims he arrived at the water meadow around eight o'clock to start work. Says he was cleaning out a ditch at the opposite end of the meadow from where Garrett's body was found. So far we just have his word for it, but he did direct us to the area in question and we were able to verify signs of fresh digging."

Powell sighed. "I hope that's the useless information."

PC Bailey grinned. "Yes, sir. The useful bit concerns Danica Hughes."

"The young woman who'd been staying with Stewart?"

"Right. Apparently he got very cagey when the subject

138

of Ms. Hughes came up. According to Sergeant Potter, it was like he was trying to protect her. He went so far as to claim he has no idea where she is."

"That seems rather unlikely, don't you think?" Powell mused.

"I'd have thought so, sir. The word is, Stewart has been carrying a torch for Ms. Hughes for years."

"Really? Ms. Hughes sounds like a most fascinating woman. She arrives in Houghton Bridge a couple of weeks ago after an absence of several years and then mysteriously disappears the day after the murder of the man widely blamed for the suicide of her best friend."

"The same thought crossed my mind, Mr. Powell."

"Does she have any family in the area?"

"Her father's in a home for the elderly in Andover, and her mum died a few years ago. She has an older sister in Australia, apparently."

"Well, it shouldn't be too hard to track her down. For starters, you could check the local post office to see if she left a forwarding address."

PC Bailey nodded.

"I'd give my eyeteeth to have a little chat with Brian Stewart," Powell continued. "However, it might be a bit difficult to arrange under the circumstances."

The young constable thought about this for a moment. "Well, sir, you can find him most evenings at the Coach and Horses."

Powell shook his head. "I'm persona non grata at that particular establishment." Then he lapsed into silence, apparently lost in thought, and it was only when the waitress arrived with their bill that he stirred. "Who is your local police surgeon, Bailey?" he asked.

"Dr. Wilson. His surgery is in the mews next to the butcher's shop."

"I assume he's the one who examined the body?"

"Yes, sir."

"I think I'll pay him a visit on my way back to Mill House."

As they prepared to leave, Powell suddenly remembered that there was something else he had forgotten to discuss with PC Bailey. He had intended to mention the rivalry between Richard Garrett and Stephen Solomon for membership in the Mayfly Club as a possible line of inquiry. He decided it could wait.

"There is one more thing, Mr. Powell," PC Bailey added by way of an afterthought.

"Yes, Bailey?"

"It turns out that Richard Garrett was murdered near the very spot Maggie Stewart hanged herself."

When eventually the door opened, Powell was confronted by a gray little man with sharp blue eyes. "Dr. Wilson, I presume?"

"The surgery is closed. Did you have an appointment?" came the brusque reply.

Charming bedside manner. "I don't require your medical services, Dr. Wilson, but I did have a few questions I was hoping you could answer."

"And your name is . . . ?"

"Powell."

"Well, Mr. Powell, you'll not be wasting any more of my time. Good day to you." He started to close the door.

"I promise I won't keep you for more than a few minutes."

Dr. Wilson examined him shrewdly. "Are you a reporter?"

Powell smiled. "You could say that I'm a historian," he answered, not without a particle of truth. Straying a little further from the straight and narrow, he went on to explain that he was conducting research on unsolved crimes in English villages.

Dr. Wilson cut him off. "I'm afraid you've come to the wrong place."

"You *are* the local police surgeon?"

"I am. But if you've come to inquire about the recent murder in the village, you'll have to talk to the police."

Powell shook his head. "Actually, I'm seeking information about a local girl named Maggie Stewart. I believe she died in Houghton Bridge some years ago. Are you familiar with the case?"

Dr. Wilson eyed him suspiciously. "You said your interest was in unsolved crimes. Maggie Stewart was a suicide, which is not a crime in the usual sense of the word."

"But an intriguing story nonetheless," Powell said quickly. "A young woman with everything to live for tragically takes her own life amidst idyllic surroundings—"

The police surgeon grimaced. "Spare me the purple prose, Mr. Powell." He hesitated, as if weighing his options. "All right," he said, "I'll answer your questions if you promise not to bother me again." He glanced at his watch. "I'll give you exactly ten minutes."

Powell waited expectantly on the doorstep.

Dr. Wilson sighed heavily. "I suppose you'd better come in."

He escorted Powell into his consulting room, which was cluttered with books and the usual medical paraphernalia, including, draped over a peg on the wall above the examination table, an ominous-looking tube with a rubber bulb attached to it.

The police surgeon examined Powell over his spectacles. "You now have nine minutes," he said.

Powell extracted his fishing diary from his jacket pocket and turned to a blank page. "To begin with, do you recall the year Maggie Stewart died?" he asked.

"Nineteen ninety-four, as I recall—I remember it was early December."

"Did you know her?"

Dr. Wilson appeared to consider this for a moment. "She was a patient of mine. Nearly everyone in Houghton Bridge has been a patient of mine at one time or another." His manner was guarded.

"Can you tell me anything about her?"

"She was a nice enough girl, from what I knew of her."

Powell began to get a sinking feeling. "How old was she when she died?"

"Eighteen."

"Was she depressed or suicidal at the time?"

"I can't say whether or not she was depressed, but she was obviously suicidal."

"I know she hanged herself beside the Houghton Brook. I am trying to understand exactly what happened."

"She took a rope, placed a noose around her neck, and tied the other end to a tree."

Powell was unsure whether the good doctor was attempting to be droll or just aggravating. "I am interested in her motivation," he persisted, "*why* she did it. I understand that this is essentially a story of unrequited love. The girl had been having an affair, became pregnant, and committed suicide after being rejected by her lover."

The police surgeon shrugged. "I really couldn't say. My field is medicine, not melodrama." He glanced significantly at his watch.

Powell probed. "I get the impression that there is some sensitivity surrounding Maggie Stewart's suicide. . . ."

Dr. Wilson looked at him, his eyes as hard as sapphires. "Her death was tragic—that goes without saying—but it happened a long time ago. Life goes on, Mr. Powell."

"Does it, Dr. Wilson?"

A shadow flickered across the police surgeon's face. He got abruptly to his feet. "I'm afraid your time is up. I'll see you out."

Powell was not so easily deterred. "Can you at least confirm that she was pregnant?" he asked.

Dr. Wilson sighed. "Yes, she was pregnant."

"Did she leave any clue to her state of mind at the time—a suicide note, perhaps?"

"She didn't leave a suicide note. Now good day to you."

When his visitor had left, Dr. Wilson returned to his surgery and sat at his desk for a moment. Then he picked up the telephone.

He fidgeted impatiently until eventually someone answered.

"Get me Inspector Marsh."

CHAPTER 20

As Powell lounged about in his room before dinner, he contemplated the not unpleasant prospect of having to serve as Jemma Walker's dogsbody tomorrow. In fishing contests, size (as they say in the adverts) does matter and he had admittedly come up a few inches short. It occurred to him that, in addition to following her around all day and netting her fish for her, he would have to lay on a decent lunch. He decided that he had better consult with Jim about this, as his own experience organizing cucumber sandwiches and petits fours for a *fête champêtre* was decidedly limited.

Just as he was considering popping downstairs to seek out his host, a nagging thought intruded. He had meant to call Sir Reginald Quick, the senior Home Office pathologist, in London to follow up on his conversation with Dr. Wilson. He checked the time and briefly considered the pros and cons of procrastinating. The last thing he wished to do was to drag Sir Reggie away from his dinner, but he knew that he probably wouldn't feel inclined to ring later. With some trepidation he placed the call.

One double ring, then a familiar bark at the other end of the line: "Quick."

"Hello, Reggie, it's Powell."

"Thank God! Here, let me take you in the study."

Powell was somewhat surprised by this reaction, since an after-hours call to Sir Reggie was normally treated as an enormous imposition. He could hear a scuffling sound and then a discordant din of voices rising to a jarring crescendo. He winced. There must be a rehearsal of the Hampstead Amateur Players in progress, in which Sir Reggie's wife was a leading light. In an act of appeasement that would have made Chamberlain blush, as Reggie himself had once put it, the pathologist had agreed to act as the company's manager and chief publicist for their main production each year. As such, he was obligated to sit through all their rehearsals, which no doubt explained why he had welcomed Powell's call as a merciful, albeit temporary deliverance.

Sir Reginald Quick was by any measure a formidable figure whose political views were slightly to the right of Lady Thatcher's. Larger than life in both physical and intellectual girth, he did not suffer fools gladly and was the bane of many a bungling policeman. And as a point of principle (although he had never articulated precisely *which* principle), he refused to be addressed by his title, which had been bestowed on him for various feats of forensic pyrotechnics.

Powell liked to think that, for the most part, he had managed to remain in the pathologist's good books, having gone out of his way over the years to cultivate the relationship. Whenever possible he made an effort to get Sir Reggie out into the field even when it wasn't absolutely necessary, as he had come to appreciate how much the pathologist relished such outings.

Eventually Powell heard the bang of a door slamming followed by a gruff voice. "Did you hear it?" Sir Reggie demanded. "It's *Les Miserables* this year, and that's exactly what they're making me. Master of the House, my arse."

Powell smiled, resisting the urge to ask what part Mrs. Quick, a force majeure in her own right, was playing. From what he knew of her, she was more Javert than Cosette. "You must reserve a pair of tickets for me," he said.

"Very funny. Now, what do you want?"

As succinctly as possible, Powell explained why he had called.

"I hadn't heard you were back at work," Sir Reggie observed warily. "What's this all about, Powell?"

Powell attempted unsuccessfully to strike a note of nonchalance. "There has been a murder, and I am trying to lend a hand, that's all."

"Ha! Has anyone actually asked you to lend a hand, as you put it? The local police, for instance?"

"Not exactly."

Sir Reggie sighed heavily. "I should have known." He sounded deflated, the prospect of an expeditious escape from eighteenth-century Paris fading fast.

"Look, Reggie, I need your help. I got the distinct impression that the local police surgeon—a Dr. Wilson—was holding something back. I can't help thinking that this chap's murder is somehow connected with the death of that girl I told you about."

"The suicide?"

"That seems to be the prevailing theory."

An ominous pause. "You don't think it was a suicide, then?"

"I'm simply trying to rule out any other possibility."

"You think she may have been murdered?"

"I don't know. I just have a feeling that there is more to it than meets the eye."

"Oh, I see!" Sir Reggie roared. "Let's all get in touch with our feelings! *Yes, M' Lord, as regards the cause of death, I have consulted my Ouija board and can report that the victim's ying was out of whack with his bloody yang!*" (Powell could well imagine the spittle flying and Sir Reggie's large moist face getting redder and redder.) "Good God, man!" the pathologist expostulated. "Have I not instilled one scintilla of the scientific method in your thinking after all these years?" It was clearly intended as a rhetorical question, because he then went off on a tangent about the decline of scientific values in modern society.

When Sir Reggie's rant had run its course, Powell got directly to the point. "I understand that the forensic science laboratory for Hampshire is in Aldermaston," he began. "Is there any way you could get access to the records relating to Maggie Stewart's death without drawing attention to the fact?"

The silence stretched out tautly for several seconds, but when Sir Reggie eventually spoke, his tone was businesslike. "I know the chap in charge over there. I'll ring him first thing Monday morning."

"Thanks, Reggie. I owe you."

"I'm putting you down for *four* tickets, by the way."

Before Powell could reply, there was a sharp exchange of voices, and Sir Reggie abruptly rang off.

The clubroom of the Mayfly Fishing Club was located on the second floor of the inn. There was a large bow window at the front, and the rear wall on either side of the brick fireplace was cluttered with paintings and photographs of past members and other assorted luminaries. Upon closer inspection, Powell concluded that one had to be dead to be thus honored. There were also half a dozen giant trout, stuffed and mounted on the wall, each with a small brass plaque commemorating the date and place of the trout's demise as well as the name of the lucky angler. In the center of the room was a long oak table where members could take their evening meal. The wall to the left of the window was lined with books. The wall opposite was taken up with a massive writing desk, above which was a double shelf full of red leather-bound ledgers—one for each decade of the club's existence—in which the vital statistics of every fish ever caught by a member of the Mayfly Club or a guest was recorded for posterity. Scattered throughout the room were several leather chairs and small round tables, like mahogany moons orbiting plush green planets, where the members could sit of an evening, drinking their whiskies, smoking their cigars, and lying about their catches.

Sir Robert Alderson, Jemma Walker's mentor and the secretary of the Mayfly Club, was tall and gray with thin shoulders that were slightly rounded from bending too long over his medical texts, one fancied. His eyes, which were gray also, radiated intelligence, and he spoke with an understated, yet unmistakable air of authority. It struck Powell that Sir Robert had that happy ability shared by all great teachers (and according to Jemma he had been one of the best) to saturate every word—chosen with an apparently unconscious attention to aptness and economy—with meaning.

Sir Robert sat at the head of the dining table with Powell and Jemma Walker on either side next to him. After passing a half hour or so engaged in small talk about Cambridge and fly fishing, Sir Robert leaned back in his chair and examined Powell thoughtfully. "Jemma's been telling me all about you, Mr. Powell," he said.

Powell smiled. "Guilty as charged, I'm afraid."

Sir Robert regarded Jemma with obvious affection. "She has spoken of you in the most glowing terms, I can assure you."

Jemma frowned in mock concentration, as if trying to recall. "To be precise, I think what I said was, 'Despite the fact he is on holiday from his job at New Scotland Yard, he can't seem to keep his nose out of local police affairs.' " She smiled innocently. "At least, I think that's how I put it."

Powell was taken aback for an instant. It occurred to

him that perhaps their casual chat over a pint hadn't been so casual after all. "I come down on the nature side of the nature-nurture question, Ms. Walker, so I suppose you could say that I'm just naturally curious."

She raised an eyebrow but did not reply.

"Precisely!" Sir Robert interjected. "And that is why I've invited you here."

Powell felt his mental antennae begin to vibrate. "Then perhaps we could get to the point . . ."

Sir Robert's expression suddenly grew serious. He regarded Powell speculatively, then appeared to come to a decision. "I would like you to find out who murdered Richard Garrett," he said.

CHAPTER 21

"I am offering you a chance to satisfy your natural curiosity and"—he glanced at Jemma—"to be of assistance to us."

"As you are no doubt aware, Sir Robert," Powell replied carefully, "the local police are looking into the matter and—"

Sir Robert gestured dismissively. "A plodding bunch, from what I know of 'em. Besides, I had something a little more . . . discreet in mind."

"I have no authority to meddle in an investigation in another jurisdiction. I'm sure you can appreciate that I could get into a lot of trouble if I did."

Sir Robert frowned. "But I thought you had expressed an interest in the case."

"Being interested is one thing, getting directly involved is quite another."

"Perhaps I could arrange it."

"What do you mean?"

"The chief constable is a friend of mine. . . ."

Powell shook his head. "I'm presently on medical leave. Even in the unlikely event that the local constabulary were to request the Yard's assistance, my superiors would never agree to let me do it. I'm sorry, Sir Robert."

The old man sighed. "I see. Well, that's that, then."

There was an awkward silence.

Jemma leaned forward and gazed at Powell across the table. "Perhaps if you knew a little more about Richard Garrett you'd agree to help."

Sir Robert clucked disapprovingly. "Now, Jemma, we don't want to get Mr. Powell in trouble with his superiors, do we?"

It was such a transparent attempt at manipulation, Powell smiled in spite of himself. He had already made up his mind in any case. "All right," he said, "I'll listen to what you both have to say. If I can help, I will. If I can't, I'll tell you."

Jemma grinned. "Right."

Sir Robert looked relieved. "Thank you, Mr. Powell, I'm in your debt."

"Not at all, Sir Robert."

Jemma got to her feet. "First off, let's dispense with the formalities." She looked from one to the other, then back again. "Bob, this is Powell. Powell, this is Bob. I'll go get us a bottle."

"Get the eighteen-year-old, Jemma," Sir Robert called after her. "Wonderful girl, brilliant mind," he added after his protégée had left the room. He looked at Powell with amusement. "You two seem to have hit it off."

"Yes, well, Jemma's a very engaging young woman," Powell answered honestly, but as he spoke the words he wondered if they would be misinterpreted. "And a much better fly fisherman than I am," he added. "But don't tell her I said that."

Sir Robert smiled. "Jemma is very single-minded about everything she does. Never had any children of my own, so I took her under my wing. She was probably one of the two or three most promising students I ever taught. Could have written her ticket at any university in the country, but she wanted to help as many people as possible in a more direct way, so she decided to start her own firm. Tell me, do you know anything about artificial—?" He stopped short. "Forgive me, Chief Superintendent, but I didn't catch your first name."

"Erskine."

"Yes, of course." Sir Robert didn't seem entirely comfortable with such informality.

Powell could sympathize, as he found it difficult to think of the celebrated surgeon as "Bob." Best just to avoid the issue altogether, he decided.

"Now then, where were we?" Sir Robert continued. "Oh yes, we were discussing the problem with artificial hearts and I was about to say that Jemma—"

"Enough shoptalk, Bob," Jemma said sternly as she returned with a sterling tray bearing the bottle of malt, three glasses, and a small bottle of springwater.

"Nonsense, Jemma," Powell rejoined. "I have an abiding interest in the human heart, in pristine condition or otherwise."

Sir Robert laughed. "I do believe that the chief superintendent is a romantic, Jemma."

Powell continued to look at Jemma as he replied, "Does that surprise you?"

Sir Robert shrugged. "I suppose it does in a way. I should have thought that a policeman's lot—exposure to life in the mean streets, as it were—would tend to engender a certain sense of realism."

Powell turned to Sir Robert. "There are two ways to look at it—at life in general, I suppose. The way it is or the way it could be." He felt Jemma's eyes on him as he spoke. He took a sip of whisky and felt the warmth spread into his chest. Nature's anesthetic for the heart, he thought.

"And how do *you* look at life in general?" she asked.

He smiled. "You haven't asked me here to bore you with my personal philosophy. Don't you think we should get down to business?"

Sir Robert nodded. "Yes—yes, of course. Where would you like me to begin?"

"Why don't you start with Richard Garrett?"

"A bright lad with a promising future. Set to take up the helm at his father's law firm one day." He shook his head. "It's tragic, simply tragic."

"I understand that his father is Bernard Garrett, the solicitor."

Sir Robert nodded. "Bernard is one of my oldest friends. An Oxford man"—he smiled faintly—"but I've never held that against him. The poor chap isn't well; I worry that the shock of Richard's death will prove to be too much for him."

"Are there any other children?"

Sir Robert shook his head. "Richard was an only child, Bernard's pride and joy."

"Where is Mr. Garrett now?"

"In London. He'll be coming down after the funeral, to scatter Richard's ashes in the Test. Richard would have wanted that."

"Richard was a keen fisherman, then?"

"Of course. He had been nominated for membership in the club this year."

Powell frowned. "I'm a bit puzzled about something. . . . I understand that Richard Garrett hadn't been back to Houghton Bridge for quite some time. To be more precise, I've been told that this was his first season in seven years. That strikes me as a bit odd, considering he was such a keen fisherman."

Sir Robert smiled crookedly. "There is no need to go all round the houses, Chief Superintendent. You've obviously been doing your homework. I imagine you want to know all about Richard Garrett and Maggie Stewart. I will oblige you, but first tell me what you know of the affair."

Powell shrugged. "The general consensus seems to be that Richard got her pregnant, then broke off the relationship, which led to her suicide a few months later."

Jemma Walker's eyes flashed angrily. "Well, the general consensus is wrong! How can you—"

"Please leave this to me, Jemma," Sir Robert interrupted. He looked at Powell. "Hear me out and then you can draw your own conclusions."

"Go on," Powell replied neutrally.

Sir Robert set his glass on the table, then leaned back in his chair. His eyes appeared to focus on something in the distance. "It was the spring of nineteen ninety-four. The mayfly was late that year, and fishing had been slow. Richard had come down from London with his father for a week. He was still at university then and used to come here quite often during the spring and summer. As it turned out, it would be Richard's last full season on the Test."

Jemma reached over with the bottle and replenished Sir Robert's glass, then looked questioningly at Powell. He shook his head.

"Which brings us to the subject of Maggie Stewart," Sir Robert continued. "Maggie was a very attractive girl, with lovely red hair, full of life. We saw quite a lot of her as she and our former riverkeeper's daughter were best friends—"

"Danica Hughes?" Powell interjected.

Sir Robert looked mildly surprised. "You continue to impress me, Chief Superintendent. Anyway, as I was saying, one thing led to another, and Richard and Maggie had a brief affair that summer. Both sowing their wild oats, I expect. It all ended amicably enough, as far as I know."

"The girl was pregnant."

"There is no evidence that Richard had anything to do with it."

Powell was about to ask the obvious question but decided to leave it for the time being. "I understand that Ms.

Hughes also chose this year to return to Houghton Bridge," he observed casually.

Sir Robert furrowed his brow. "Yes, Danica arrived a couple of weeks ago. I believe she is staying with Maggie's brother, Brian."

"She *was* staying with Maggie's brother."

"I beg your pardon?"

"She seems to have disappeared."

"Really?"

"Were you aware that Brian Stewart was taken in for questioning about Garrett's murder?"

"I did hear something about it."

"Isn't it reasonable to assume that both Danica Hughes and Brian Stewart blame Garrett for Maggie's death?"

"It's still a free country, Chief Superintendent."

"Is there anything else you want to tell me?"

"I think I've given you the gist of it."

Powell drained his glass and got to his feet. "I'm sorry, Sir Robert, but I'm afraid I can't help you." He turned to Jemma. "I assume we're still on for tomorrow?"

She was staring at Sir Robert. "Bob, you must tell him everything."

Sir Robert sighed heavily.

There was a sudden fierce rattle of rain against the window. Jemma got up and drew the curtains. "It's pouring cats and dogs," she said. Then she looked at Powell. "I think we can forget about tomorrow."

CHAPTER 22

"I got the whole story from Bernard," Sir Robert began. "I had no reason to doubt the truth of it then, nor, even in light of recent events, do I doubt it now. This sordid business is a testament to his son's character, not an indictment. It is true that Richard had an affair with Maggie Stewart. More accurately, the lad was head over heels in love with her. It is difficult to put into words exactly, but Maggie had a certain joie de vivre that was irresistible. Anyway, they were inseparable that summer, but when it came time for Richard to return to university, they decided to go their separate ways. According to Bernard, it was Maggie's decision. Richard, however, continued to carry a torch for the girl." Sir Robert paused to stare into his glass, swirling the amber liquid round and round. He looked up presently. "So you can appreciate, Chief Superintendent, that when news came of Maggie's suicide, Richard was devastated."

"Is that why he stayed away from Houghton Bridge for all those years?"

Sir Robert nodded. "Too many painful memories, I imagine, not to mention the almost universal hostility of the villagers to contend with. He was only human, after all."

"What about the pregnancy?"

"It only came to light as a result of the postmortem examination. According to Bernard, Richard swore that he was not the father but, in consideration of Maggie's memory, he refused to deny it publicly. He didn't want to appear spiteful, nor, I should imagine, did he wish to draw attention to the fact that Maggie had got herself involved with another man. I suppose that's understandable."

Powell was skeptical. "How could he know for certain that he wasn't the father?"

"I really couldn't say."

Powell persisted. "Do you know if he had any idea who it might have been?"

"If he did, Bernard never mentioned it."

"I wonder why they broke it off?" Powell mused.

"I beg your pardon?"

"Why Maggie decided to end the affair. You said they were inseparable that summer—one can only assume that she was in love with him as well."

Sir Robert shrugged. "I don't pretend to understand the vagaries of the human heart, Chief Superintendent," he said, seemingly unaware of the irony. "Who can say? Richard was returning to Oxford, and long-distance romances can be difficult. . . ." He trailed off.

"What did Richard's father think of the relationship?"

Sir Robert looked slightly uncomfortable. "I don't think he was too keen on it. He had great plans for Richard, and I suspect he had a more . . . advantageous union in mind for his son. Bernard is a little old-fashioned in some ways," he added, as if by way of an excuse.

"Was Maggie aware of his feelings?"

"I have no idea."

At this point, Jemma Walker jumped in. "I don't see that her reasons for breaking up with Richard have anything to do with his murder."

"On the contrary, it seems to me that it raises all sorts of interesting possibilities. For instance, if Maggie Stewart broke up with Garrett because of another man, it would certainly cast a different light on her suicide—if that's in fact what it was."

It was as if Powell had detonated a bomb, scattering speculative shrapnel in all directions.

"What do you mean?" Sir Robert reacted sharply before being interrupted by Jemma Walker.

"You think she was murdered?" she asked incredulously.

Powell shrugged. "There is no reason to think it was anything other than suicide at this point. I am simply saying that one must reexamine one's assumptions when the context changes. If Bernard Garrett's account of events is nearer to the truth than the popular version, then we've gone from the suicide of a jilted lover to . . . something else perhaps."

"Wait a minute," Jemma protested. "Even if there was another man, Maggie's motivation for killing herself may still have been the same."

"True enough. But then whoever killed Richard Garrett—assuming his murder was an act of revenge for Maggie's death—got the wrong man."

Jemma looked at Sir Robert, who appeared to be off in his own world. "Bob?" she prompted gently.

"What? Yes, well, I was just thinking—it's probably nothing, but, shortly after he arrived, Richard did get into a heated argument with Simon Street of Houghton Manor." He looked at Powell. "Have you met the gentleman?"

Powell grimaced. "I've had the pleasure."

Sir Robert nodded. "A nasty piece of work, that one. And an indifferent fisherman besides," he added disdainfully. "In any event, Richard encountered him while fishing one day, and Street began to go on about the club's lease, accusing us of stealing the bread off his table or some such rubbish. To make a long story short, he indicated that he intended to sell the estate along with the fishing rights, which would certainly complicate matters for the club. I didn't think much of it at the time since Street has made similar threats to other members recently. And in any case, Mrs. Street makes such decisions."

"Why don't you tell me about Mrs. Street."

"Lovely person. As was her late husband, Colonel Waddington. It was a great blow to the village when Colonel Waddington died." Sir Robert frowned. "Unfortunately, Pamela took up with Simon Street shortly afterward."

"As a matter of interest, how did Colonel Waddington die?"

"Drowned while fishing. The old boy was getting on, and apparently lost his footing wading across the stream, banged his head on a rock, and that was it."

Powell considered this for a moment. "How in heaven's name did Mrs. Street ever get tied up with Simon?"

Sir Robert shook his head sadly. "Who can blame her, really. It is difficult enough to traverse this vale of tears, let alone solo. The colonel was considerably older than she was, and one gets the impression that she relied on him a great deal to manage their affairs." He shot Jemma a meaningful look. "And while I know it is not politically correct to say so, I think she simply missed having a man about the house."

Powell noticed with some amusement that the bait floated past Jemma, unmolested, like one of his Iron Blue Duns.

"Apparently she met Street at some social function in London," Sir Robert continued. "He was in a play in the West End at the time and was no doubt at his charming best. And although Pamela is several years older than Street, it must be said that she is a very attractive woman."

"Do you know if they met before or after the colonel died?"

Sir Robert seemed surprised by the question. "I honestly don't know."

"Go on."

"There's not much more to tell, really. To put it bluntly,

Simon found himself a meal ticket and Pamela another man. Although I often wonder if she had it to do over again . . ." He hesitated.

"What do you mean?"

"I can't put my finger on it exactly"—he frowned—"whenever I see her, she seems . . . subdued somehow, not her old self. In fact I hardly ever see her in the village anymore."

Powell nodded. Time now to begin grappling with the main problem. "I'd like to fast-forward to Thursday morning," he said. "I understand that Garrett was fishing near the weir on the Houghton Brook. Is that right?"

Sir Robert nodded. "We refer to the stretch from the weir downstream to Test as the Weir Beat. The stretch upstream to the bridge is known as the Bridge Beat. Richard was fishing below the weir that morning."

"Did anyone talk to him before he set out?"

Sir Robert shook his head. "He must have left early. I didn't see him at breakfast."

"I had dinner with him the night before, in Stockbridge," Jemma chimed in. "There was Stephen Solomon, Richard, and me."

"Really?" A surprisingly genial rivalry amongst the candidates for the Mayfly Club membership, Powell thought, considering the stakes. "How did Richard seem to you?"

She shrugged. "Fine. Of course I didn't really know him that well."

"I want you to think carefully: Did he say anything or

give any indication that something might be bothering him?"

She frowned. "It's funny you should mention it but he did bring up the business of Simon Street and the fish—you know, the poaching incident I told you about."

"There was never any proof, Jemma," Sir Robert cautioned.

Jemma ignored him. "The thing was, although Richard recounted the story in a humorous way—it *was* only a fish, after all—I got the distinct impression that he still held it against Street. I can't explain it exactly—but there was definitely an undercurrent there."

Powell nodded. The room fell silent except for the ticking of a clock, which, oddly enough, he hadn't noticed before. He mulled over the various possibilities, from the most likely to the highly improbable, before ending up, vaguely dissatisfied, back where he had started.

"Well, Chief Superintendent?" Sir Robert was saying.

Powell couldn't help noticing that Jemma was watching him expectantly. "From a purely objective point of view," he said presently, "I think that the most plausible explanation is still the conventional one. Maggie Stewart, who was carrying Richard Garrett's child, was disconsolate over their breakup and tragically took her own life. However—"

"You can't be serious!" Jemma objected. "Haven't you heard a word we've said? It's obvious you'd rather believe a bunch of village busybodies!"

"Bernard Garrett may well believe that his son was not

responsible for the girl's death," Powell continued patiently. "Even if Richard did feel in some way responsible, it wouldn't be particularly surprising if he didn't admit it to his father."

Jemma was about to protest further, but Sir Robert interjected. "I believe you were about to qualify your conclusion, Chief Superintendent."

"I have to admit that one thing is still bothering me. Why did Richard Garrett choose this particular time to return to Houghton Bridge, after so many years avoiding the place?"

"Time heals all wounds, Chief Superintendent. I suspect that his nomination for membership in the club, coupled with a desire to get on with his life—to use the current vernacular—were responsible for his decision."

"Perhaps," Powell replied. "But it strikes me as rather odd that Danica Hughes decided almost simultaneously to do the same thing."

CHAPTER 23

The next morning dawned damp and dreary and Powell had come to a decision of his own. For a number of reasons he had decided it was time to return to London. He had imposed on his host for far too long; his interest in the Garrett case was flagging—or rather he had accepted the fact that he was not in a position to pursue it any further; and he could no longer ignore the reality that he had his own house to put in order. Jemma Walker had informed him last night that she was also leaving today, and they had made a vague arrangement to get together sometime for a day's fishing. But Powell had already concluded, for all the obvious reasons, that this was a commitment that would likely remain unconsummated.

He had made a list of things he needed to do before he left and reckoned that if all went according to plan, he should be able to catch a late train back to London. As luck would have it, he had been lumbered with the

Dorkings again at breakfast, so he wasn't able to inform Jim Hardy of his plans.

As Powell collapsed his umbrella and boarded the Stockbridge bus, he was slightly surprised to see that there was only one other passenger on the bus—an elderly woman staring straight ahead clutching an empty shopping bag. As Powell took his seat, a young woman, appearing slightly flushed and out of breath, got on, hurried past, and sat down behind him.

Powell's impressions during the ten-minute ride were of drab green countryside punctuated with occasional muddy farmsteads glimpsed through the rain-blurred windows. He got off in the High Street and set out in search of the local fishing shop, where he intended to buy a fishing reel for Jim Hardy as a small token of his appreciation. As he was about to cross the road, he heard a feminine voice behind him.

"Excuse me."

He turned. It was the young woman from the bus. She brushed the long hair from her eyes. Her face was pale and anxious.

"Mr. Powell?"

He smiled reassuringly. "Yes. Can I help you?"

"My name is Danica Hughes. I'm sorry for bothering you, but I—I was wondering if we could talk. . . ."

Powell felt a surge of excitement. "Of course, Ms. Hughes," he replied as casually as he could manage under the circumstances. "What did you have in mind?"

She looked relieved. "There's a coffee shop in the hotel. It should be open by now. We could go there."

"Lead the way, Ms. Hughes."

* * *

It occurred to Powell that Danica Hughes, who appeared at first glance to be a rather ordinary young woman, was really quite extraordinary. Her complexion was pale like porcelain, quintessentially English, and her manner was reserved. But there was something else beneath the surface that hinted at a passionate nature. Sitting across the table from him, she looked nervous but determined.

It was still early and they had the restaurant to themselves. Powell waited for their waiter to disappear before getting down to business. "Now then, Ms. Hughes, to what do I owe this pleasure?" he asked.

"It's Danica."

"That's a lovely name. *Ephemera danica.*"

She looked mildly surprised. "That's very good, Mr. Powell."

"I like to do my homework."

"But what exactly is your assignment? That's what I've been asking myself."

"I might ask you the same thing. For starters, how did you know who I was?"

"It's all over the village, has been from the day you arrived. Mrs. Fielding at Mill House has never met a secret she wasn't willing to introduce to everyone in the village."

Powell cursed to himself. That explained a few things. "I didn't realize I was such a celebrity," he said. "Here I thought I was just an overworked policeman on holiday."

"Which brings us to the subject of Richard Garrett's murder."

Powell studied his companion's face. "Well, Danica, I

won't deny that you've piqued my interest. Please continue."

"I've heard that you've been making certain inquiries and it occurred to me that perhaps you could help me."

"I'm not sure I understand. . . ."

"It concerns a friend of mine, Brian Stewart. I'm worried sick about him. I've been staying with Brian since—" She checked herself. "Perhaps I should explain. I'm from Houghton Bridge originally, but I've—I've been away. I only just got back a few weeks ago." She hesitated. "The thing is, the police have questioned Brian about Richard's murder, and I want you to know that he had nothing to do with it."

Powell looked doubtful. "Why would you possibly care what I think? You must know that I have no official status here."

"That's just it, you have no ax to grind, and say what you want about Mrs. Fielding, she's a good judge of character and she says you're a decent bloke."

"I must get her to write a letter of commendation to my superiors," Powell quipped.

"This is serious!"

"Murder is always serious, Danica. As serious as it gets. Which makes me wonder why you are attempting to shield your friend."

She attempted unsuccessfully to affect an offhand manner. "What do you mean? Brian is harmless. He wouldn't hurt a fly."

"Why did you leave him to the wolves, then?"

She stared at him in disbelief. "You have no right to—"

"Isn't it true that you left Brian a note telling him you were going away?"

"Yes, I ran away"—her eyes brimmed with tears—"because I couldn't bloody take any more!" She began to sob quietly.

Powell felt a stab of guilt. The girl was clearly on the edge emotionally, yet he was treating her as if she had been tried and found guilty of something. "Forgive me, Danica. It's just that everybody seems to want my advice but nobody seems willing to tell me the bloody truth." She looked up, and he handed her a napkin.

She dabbed at her eyes.

"I'll make you a promise," he continued against his better judgment. "If you tell me everything you know about this business, I'll do my best to get to the bottom of it. All right?"

She smiled faintly and nodded.

"If I seem a bit direct in my questioning it's only because I need to—"

She interrupted him. "It's okay, really, I understand."

"Right." He took a moment to formulate his thoughts. No point in going all round the houses, he decided. "Would I be totally wide of the mark," he asked, "if I were to assume that your first thought when you heard that Garrett had been murdered was that Brian Stewart had something to do with it?"

"That was my second thought, actually. My first thought was that Richard Garrett had finally got what he'd deserved." She returned his gaze unwaveringly. "I don't imagine I need to explain it to you, do I?"

"I think you'd better."

She shrugged. "Once upon a time there was a beautiful princess named Maggie who lived beside a magical river. Her best friend was a fairy mayfly named Danica. But one day, Maggie met an evil prince who charmed her, used her, and then discarded her. Brokenhearted, the beautiful princess decided to kill herself, and not even the fairy mayfly could save her." She looked at Powell. "The End." Her voice was matter-of-fact, devoid of emotion.

Powell could think of nothing to say.

"After the initial reaction," she continued, "my feelings were more along the lines of relief. For the past seven years I'd lived with the reality of Maggie's death—every single day—and I'd reached the point where I could no longer deal with it. So I suppose I viewed Richard's death as a sort of closure. But the thing is, I've come to realize that there will never be any end to it. As long as I live, I will never be able to forgive myself." She hesitated for a moment. "The day Maggie died, she called me and asked me if I wanted to go down to London with her for the day. She said she needed to get away. I told her I couldn't because I'd made plans to be with John—my boyfriend at the time." She swallowed. "So you see, if I hadn't been so selfish . . . well, it might have turned out differently."

"You mustn't blame yourself."

"Who *should* I blame then?"

Before Powell could reply, she continued. "This isn't about me, Mr. Powell. It's Brian I'm worried about. That's the only reason I'm here now—to do what I can to help him."

"Why do you suppose the police took him in for questioning?"

"It's obvious. They suspect him of killing Richard."

"Maybe he did."

"I told you before," she said, an edge of exasperation in her voice, "Brian isn't capable of harming anyone. Except perhaps himself."

"Tell me about him."

She appeared to choose her words carefully. "Brian is very sensitive . . . emotionally fragile, you might say. Even when he was younger—before Maggie's death, I mean—he was prone to bouts of depression. As is often the case with people like that, he's very creative. He wanted to be a writer once but never got around to it, I guess. Now he digs ditches for the local council. He and Maggie were very close, and since she died it's—it's been very difficult for Brian. He's on antidepressants and drinks quite a lot, and I sensed from his recent letters that he was getting worse. That's the reason I decided to come back to Houghton Bridge."

"Are you aware that he had an altercation with Richard Garrett in the village High Street the day before the murder?"

She sighed. "It wouldn't surprise me."

"You indicated that Brian isn't capable of murder. How can you be so sure?"

She answered without hesitation. "I think most people are capable of just about anything, don't you? You must see it every day in your job. And you only have to look around at what's happening in the world today. But even if Brian had considered taking revenge on Richard, I think there's something that would have held him back in the end."

"Yes?"

"Me. He's in love with me, or at least he thinks he is. Poor bastard."

"I think you do yourself a disservice, Danica."

"Do you? The point is, I know Brian would never do anything to make me unhappy."

"Perhaps he thought that killing Garrett would make you happy."

"I would be unhappy for Brian."

"Are you in love with him?"

"Not in the sense you mean. Brian and I have always been close—" she hesitated "—I know he has feelings for me, but I think of him more as a big brother."

"Danica, you know the players in this piece as well as anyone. If Brian didn't kill Garrett, do you have any idea who did?"

She regarded him coolly. "Does that mean you've crossed me off your list?"

Powell refused to bite.

"Well, just in case you *are* wondering," she continued, "I had as much reason to hate Richard Garrett as anyone but I draw the line short of murder." Then she paused, as if considering the implications of Powell's question. "I'm sorry," she said eventually, "I really couldn't say who murdered Richard."

CHAPTER 24

As the waiter replenished their coffees, Powell experienced a growing sense of frustration. He was still not able to reconcile the two opposing views of Maggie Stewart and Richard Garrett's relationship—or rather how it had ended. More to the point, there was no proof that there was even a connection between any of this and Garrett's murder. Before he traveled any farther down that particular speculative road, he needed to get it straight in his own mind. His instincts told him that the nature of their relationship lay at the heart of the case, and he decided to press Danica Hughes a little harder.

She brushed the hair nervously from her face, as if she were reading his thoughts.

"What would you say," he said, "if I told you I had it on good authority that it was Maggie who ended her relationship with Richard and not the other way around?"

Her eyes flashed angrily. "I'd say you'd better check your source. It's simply not true."

"How do you know it isn't true?"

"She was my best friend."

"Then she talked to you about Richard?"

"Why is this relevant?"

Powell did his best to explain.

"Look, Mr. Powell, I have no idea why Richard was murdered. All I know is what he did to Maggie. End of story."

"Is it?"

"What do you mean?"

"Either Richard's death is related to his relationship with Maggie or it isn't. Personally, I don't believe in coincidences. The easy explanation is that someone blamed him for Maggie's death and acted out of revenge. There is, however, another possibility." He paused.

"I'm dying to hear it," she said.

"What did Maggie tell you at the time that she and Richard broke up?"

She sighed. "She said they both agreed it was best. It was the end of the summer, Richard had to leave to go back to university, and neither of them wanted to be tied down."

"Did you believe her?"

"I had no reason not to at the time."

"What changed your mind?"

"When I found out she was pregnant."

"And when was that?"

She swallowed. "After she was—it all came out at the coroner's inquest. I didn't know before."

Powell nodded, considering his next question. "Have

you ever considered the possibility," he said gently, "that Richard Garrett wasn't the father?"

"What are you suggesting?" she shot back angrily. "That Maggie slept around?"

"I wasn't suggesting—"

"If she'd had another boyfriend, I would have known about it. I'll tell you exactly what happened," she continued bitterly, cutting off Powell's response. "Richard thought he was too good for her. He had his fancy legal career to think about and didn't want to be saddled with a simple county wife and child." She was growing increasingly agitated. "And I'll tell you something else, Mr. Powell: Maggie loved life more than anyone I've ever known. And she was more than capable of dealing with anything that came her way. If she had decided to keep the baby she'd have put her heart and soul into being the best mother in the world—that's the type of person she was." Danica's eyes glistened. "If you don't believe me, ask your friend Jim Hardy. Maggie worked at Mill House for a while.

"I won't say I wasn't worried about her when she and Richard broke up," she continued. "Maggie tended to be a bit impetuous—she often did things on the spur of the moment." Danica stared defiantly at Powell. "But there is no way," she said, "no bloody way in the world that Maggie would ever have taken her own life."

By the time Powell got back to Houghton Bridge, the rain was pelting down and a few churchgoers straggled down Church Hill after morning service. An elderly man peering warily from under his umbrella gave him a perfunctory nod as they passed. As he climbed the hill toward the stone tower of St. Andrew's, which seemed overwhelmed by the wet gray sky, he puzzled once again over something that had been bothering him from the start. Why had the tragic, but hardly unprecedented, death of a young woman so many years ago had such a lingering impact on the lives of people in the village? Suicides happen every day, particularly among young people who, superficially at least, had bright futures ahead of them. He shook his head as if trying to clear the clutter from his mind.

On the question of Maggie Stewart's relationship with Richard Garrett, he was inclined to give some weight to the view of Sir Robert Alderson, which had also been hinted at by the vicar. That is, that young Garrett was truly in love with the girl, but for some reason (perhaps the one she had given to Danica Hughes), she had decided to end it. There was at least some evidence for this, albeit of the hearsay variety, based on Sir Robert's discussions with Richard's father. Admittedly, however, Bernard Garrett could not be relied upon to be entirely objective about his son's motivation and behavior.

The contrary case put forward by Danica Hughes (and held by just about everyone else in the village, it seemed, including Maggie's uncle, the proprietor of the Coach and Horses) was largely circumstantial. Despite the explanation given by Maggie herself, it was clear that most people viewed the end of her relationship with Garrett, her secret pregnancy, and subsequent death as causally linked. As Powell mulled this over it suddenly occurred to him that he had been overlooking something obvious, and he made a mental note to bring it up with Reggie when he talked to him tomorrow.

Changing mental gears, Powell thought about the conjunction of events that had brought both Richard Garrett and Danica Hughes back to Houghton Bridge after so many years. Richard Garrett had been nominated for membership in the Mayfly Club and, according to Sir Robert Alderson, was keen to get on with his life. For her part, Danica Hughes had said that she was worried about the increasingly precarious mental state of Maggie's brother, Brian, for whom she evidently felt some responsibility.

Powell frowned as he reflected on his conversation with Danica Hughes. She had been the first to openly suggest that perhaps Maggie Stewart's death hadn't been a suicide after all, which, if true, certainly opened up the field. And begged the obvious question, which would likely take considerably more time and resources than he had at his disposal to sort out. He cursed aloud, then felt a twinge of guilt when he realized he was standing in front of the churchyard gate.

As he rang the vicarage doorbell, he realized that he had set himself a particularly difficult nut to crack: the issue of confidentiality between a minister and one of his parishioners. Presently the door opened to reveal the Reverend Norris. He looked preoccupied but he perked up when he recognized Powell. "Erskine, this *is* an unexpected pleasure!"

"Hello, Geoffrey. May I have a word?"

An odd expression flickered across the vicar's face. "Y-yes, of course. Here, let me take your coat before you catch your death. Then I'll make us a nice cup of tea."

Powell collapsed his dripping umbrella and stepped into the hall. "That sounds like just what the doctor ordered."

A few minutes after Powell had settled himself in the sitting room, the vicar appeared with the tea and a plate of biscuits.

"I didn't see you at s-service this morning," he observed matter-of-factly as he handed Powell his cup.

"Yes, well, I'm afraid I don't get to church as often as I should."

The vicar smiled. "Well, I wouldn't w-worry about it if I were you. The good Lord has a way of letting one know when it's time."

Powell took a deep breath. "Geoffrey, I've come for your advice on a rather sensitive matter. . . ."

The vicar looked concerned. "Of course, Erskine, I'll do anything I can to help—anything at all."

"I've taken it upon myself to look a little further into Richard Garrett's murder. I think the police may be on the wrong track," he continued without going into details, "and I would like to do what I can to help put things right. The thing is, I have no jurisdiction in Houghton Bridge and I have absolutely no business getting involved in a local police matter. So you see, Geoffrey, I am on the horns of an ethical dilemma: Do I do what I think is right, or do I render unto Caesar, so to speak?"

Without hesitating, the vicar replied, "I believe your clear duty is to do what you believe to be right."

"Then I'll need your help, Geoffrey."

The vicar nodded solemnly.

Powell set his cup down on the saucer. "First off, I need to know more about Pamela and Simon Street. From what little I know of them, they strike me as rather an odd couple."

"Before we go any further, Erskine, we need to set the ground rules for this c-conversation. As I've told you before, parishioners frequently come to me in confidence to discuss various p-personal issues. Much as I'd like to help you, I am not prepared to betray that trust. However, I will try to answer your questions as best I can. But you must understand that there is a line that I simply cannot cross."

"I understand, of course."

The vicar reflected for a moment, shaking his head sadly. "What can I tell you about Pamela Street? A wonderful woman. Generous to a fault, as was her late husband. Unfortunately, she has grown increasingly unhappy since Colonel Waddington died and, in recent years, even reclusive. And if I may be completely frank with you, Erskine, I believe that Simon Street is largely r-responsible."

"How so?"

"Mr. Street has taken to managing the affairs of the estate and is constantly raising the specter of financial ruin if Mrs. Street doesn't do as he wishes."

"Such as selling the Manor?"

The vicar nodded bleakly.

"How much influence do you think Street ultimately has over Pamela?"

The vicar deliberated for a few seconds before replying. "If you're asking me whether she will eventually go along with him, I couldn't really say. What I do know is that she is worried half to death about losing the estate and everything she and Colonel Waddington w-worked so hard to build up."

"Is it possible," Powell asked, "that Mr. Street is acting legitimately in what he believes to be Pamela's best interests?"

"I hope you don't think it uncharitable of me for saying so, but I have reluctantly come to the conclusion that Mr. Street's only concern is for himself."

Powell hesitated. "I don't know exactly how to put this, Geoffrey, but do you suppose there is anything that Street might do to cause Pamela to assert herself?"

"I'm not quite sure I understand you."

"I assume from what you've told me that Mrs. Street still calls the shots at Houghton Manor, and Simon Street serves at her pleasure, as it were. I'm just wondering what it would take for him to wear out his welcome—for Mrs. Street to finally get fed up with his carryings-on and chuck him out on his ear."

"I suppose it would depend on the n-n-nature of the transgression."

"Poaching a trout that didn't belong to him, for instance," Powell suggested. Then he remembered the drunken young woman Street had ogled that day at the Coach and Horses. "Or womanizing."

"I r-really couldn't say," the vicar replied uncomfortably.

Time now, Powell thought, to turn from Simon Street's Svengali to Maggie Stewart, who played the lead role in this tragedy but whose character remained maddeningly elusive. He leaned forward in his chair and regarded the Reverend Geoffrey Norris with some trepidation. The vicar was his best and last chance to unravel the mystery of Maggie Stewart's death, and he knew that he only had one shot at it. The warm and heavy silence was punctuated by the ticking of a clock, and the seconds seemed to stretch out, creating a sense of urgency, a feeling of time counting down.

"I'd like to ask you now," he began carefully, "about Maggie Stewart. Did you know her?"

"She attended church from time to time—fairly regularly, in fact, for a young person these days."

Powell summarized for the vicar what he'd learned about her so far, ending up with the opposing views of her relationship with Richard Garrett. "So you see, Geoffrey, I'm left wondering why she would go to the extreme of taking her own life when she appeared to have other options. Leaving aside the conventional wisdom for a moment, it seems likely that Richard Garrett would have supported her in some fashion. Or she could simply have ended the pregnancy." He paused to gauge the vicar's reaction.

The Reverend Norris smiled faintly. "From one extreme to the other, you mean. Don't worry, Erskine, I have no intention of getting embroiled in a discussion of the abortion issue with you. I can tell you this, however: After a great deal of soul-searching, Maggie decided to keep the b-baby. She was of course hoping for some assistance from the father, but alas it was not to be. . . ." He trailed off significantly.

"When we last talked, you told me that Richard Garrett was an honorable man—I believe those were your words. Are you telling me now that he refused to help her?"

The vicar did not answer immediately. He stared at the cup and saucer resting on his lap for a considerable period of time. When he looked up his eyes were weary, but his voice was oddly matter-of-fact. "Under the circumstances, I think something a little s-stronger is in order. Sherry? Whisky?"

"Whatever you're having."

"Right." He got to his feet and walked over to a small cabinet upon which was a decanter and two sherry glasses on a sterling tray. He filled the two glasses with studied deliberation, then returned and offered one to Powell before setting the tray on the coffee table and re-settling himself in his chair. He picked up his own glass. "Cheers," he said absently before draining it in one gulp.

Powell followed suit and waited for the Reverend Norris to take the next step.

The vicar topped up their glasses before speaking. "You must understand, Erskine, that I am sailing into d-dangerous waters here. There is a fine line between helping you in your quest for the truth and descending into the realm of unethical behavior. To return to your original question, I've no doubt Richard would have supported Maggie any way he could, financially and emotionally . . . but the thing is, she didn't ask him for help." He sighed heavily. "You see, Erskine, Richard Garrett was not the father."

CHAPTER 25

Powell considered the implications of the revelation, now corroborated by the vicar, that Richard Garrett was not the father of Maggie Stewart's unborn child, which of course begged the obvious question. Powell hadn't expected the Reverend Geoffrey Norris to divulge the identity of the real father, although he suspected the vicar knew who it was. It was entirely plausible that Maggie Stewart had confided in him when she discovered she was pregnant. The really interesting question was who else knew.

The rain had let up and Powell hurried back to Mill House. As he crossed the High Street near the Mayfly Inn, he noticed a man who had just emerged from the inn suddenly turn and duck back inside as if he was trying to avoid him. The man looked familiar and it suddenly dawned on Powell that it was Stephen Soloman, the third candidate in the Mayfly Club membership election.

He was still puzzling over this when he got back to the

guesthouse. When he met Jim Hardy in the front hall, he came to a quick decision. "Jim, could I have a word?"

Hardy seemed somewhat taken aback by this request and glanced at his watch, as if doing a quick mental calculation. "No problem, there's only you and I for lunch today and the new batch of guests shouldn't start arriving until later this afternoon." He accompanied Powell into the private sitting room. "What's up?"

"I've a favor to ask of you, Jim, but first off, I wanted to tell you that I can't thank you enough for having me—it's been bloody marvelous, just what I needed to get back on my feet. If you ever need to get away and want to come down to London, we'll put you up and show you the sights. What do you say?"

Hardy sighed. "I just might take you up on that—I could use a break. Now then, you mentioned a favor?"

Powell quickly brought Hardy up-to-date on the results of his inquiries.

Hardy looked surprised. "You *have* been busy," he said.

"The thing is, Jim, something has come up and I'd like to stay another day or so—I mean, if it's all right—"

"Stay as long as you wish," Hardy interjected sternly. "And not another word about it."

Powell smiled. "Right." Then his expression grew serious. "I'd like to ask you a few questions about Maggie Stewart. I understand she used to work for you."

Hardy nodded. "She worked here briefly one summer as a chambermaid. She used to do the odd housekeeping job around the village. Why do you ask?"

"Do you know if she ever worked up at the Manor?"

He frowned. "Now that you mention it, I think she did. You could check with Pamela Street."

Powell nodded. Then he summarized his conversation with Danica Hughes that morning. "The bottom line is," he concluded, "she maintains that Maggie Stewart was not the sort of person to take her own life. I was wondering what you thought."

"I was as surprised as everyone else at the time," Hardy replied after thinking about it for a moment. "Maggie had everything going for her—looks, personality, the whole package. But when the full story eventually came out, it began to make sense and I must admit I never really questioned it. But thinking about it now, it does seem rather out of character. I mean, Maggie was the type of girl who seemed to take everything in her stride." He looked at Powell. "But then I suppose one never really knows what demons dwell beneath the surface. . . ." He lapsed into a pensive silence.

Powell got the distinct impression that there was something worrying him. "Something on your mind, Jim?" he asked.

Hardy did not speak for several seconds. When he looked up, his expression was desolate. "Erskine, I—I've done something very stupid. I've tried to forestall something I have no control over, and now I've only made things worse."

He went on to recount the details of his telephone conversation with Simon Street. "So you see I threatened the man with blackmail because I'm at the end of my bloody rope."

"You are referring, I take it, to the poaching incident?"

Hardy nodded. "I told Street I was out walking along the stream that evening and saw him let his line drift down under the bridge and hook the fish."

"Did you?"

Hardy looked sheepish. "I made it all up."

Powell was puzzled. "I don't understand—just about everyone in Houghton Bridge already thinks Street did it, so what could you possibly hope to gain?"

Hardy shook his head in disgust. "God only knows. I obviously wasn't thinking clearly."

"I assume this has something to do with losing your fishing rights."

Hardy nodded.

"But there must be something in your tenancy agreement that prevents the Manor from arbitrarily canceling it."

"There is, unless the estate is sold. Then the agreement is null and void and would have to be renegotiated with the new owner, who could choose not to let the fishing. Or increase the rent to fair market value, which is ten times what I pay now. Either way I'd have to pack up and sell Mill House."

"You know, Jim," Powell observed absently, "it strikes me that old Simon is emerging as something of a common denominator in the equation."

Hardy frowned. "I'm not sure I follow you."

"It's hard to avoid the conclusion that Street is basically a gold digger, who exerts an increasingly unhealthy influence on his wife, upon whom he depends for financial support. He had an altercation with Richard Garrett on the riverbank shortly before Garrett's murder, and it now turns out that Maggie Stewart used to be in the employ of Houghton Manor." He looked at Hardy.

Hardy looked doubtful. "Much as I'd like to fan the flames of your suspicion—God knows I'd give the world to see the bastard squirm—I can't think of many people in Houghton Bridge who *haven't* had a run-in with Street at one time or another. And as I said before, Maggie Stewart did housekeeping for a number of people in the village."

"Nonetheless," Powell replied. "I think it's time I had a little chat with Pamela Street."

"Good luck getting past Simon."

"Do you think you could arrange something?"

Hardy thought about this for a moment. "I'll see what I can do."

"Right." Powell got to his feet and glanced out the window. "It looks like the rain has let up," he observed. "I think I'll go fishing. I suspect it may be the last chance I get." In this, he was unknowingly prescient.

As Powell strolled along the bank of the Houghton Brook there were patches of blue overhead, and the sun glinted through the clouds from time to time, presaging at least a temporary lull in the rain. The *Ranunculus* was in full bloom now, dotting the surface of the stream with galaxies of tiny white flowers. The water rushed and murmured, warblers chattered in the trees, and the air was heavy with that heady smell of damp soil and green growth that follows a spring rain.

As Powell put up his rod, he noticed a few small olives were coming off, so he decided to forgo his trusty Iron Blue Dun and try a number 16 Adams, which more closely resembled the hatching fly. As he tied the fly onto his leader, he heard a splash and looked up. The telltale rings spreading in the center of the stream about twenty yards upstream indicated a good fish.

When his tackle was in order, he crouched down and made his way carefully along the bank until he was about ten yards below the spot where the trout had risen. He adjusted the Polaroid glasses on his nose and searched the water for signs of his quarry. At first glance the stream bottom appeared to be uniformly pebbled and devoid of life. And there didn't appear to be any cover sufficient to conceal a trout of any size. The only signs of movement were the subtle shadows flickering over the pebbles caused by tiny variations in the current. Powell stared at the spot where the fish had risen, or rather tried to stare through it, focusing at a point below the streambed, so as not to prejudge the trout's whereabouts.

Like the sudden apprehension of a 3-D image hidden in one of those computer-generated posters, it jumped out at him. A lighter patch of gravel, a small area of the streambed rubbed clean of silt by the trout's belly as it held itself against the current. And then miraculously, as if conjured out of thin air, a dark torpedo shape appeared, wavering in the stream like a thought suspended in the depths of consciousness.

Powell worked out a suitable length of line with a number of false casts. As the line flicked back and forth above the stream, he prayed that the shadow of the line on the water would not put the fish down. With a final forward snap of his rod he cast the fly line onto the water, placing the gossamer leader with his fly attached about ten feet upstream of the fish. Not daring to breathe, he watched the fly float downstream with the current. He drew in the line at exactly the same pace so that it would neither retard nor hasten the natural drift of the fly.

The trout rose deliberately, almost nonchalantly, to inspect the fly and then, in a great swirl, engulfed it. Powell's rod bent double and his reel screamed as the fish, pricked by the hook, tore off line. It was without a doubt the best chalk stream trout he had ever hooked, but he tried not to think about that as he focused on the task at hand. For once, everything went his way and, after a few anxious moments coaxing the trout out of a weedbed it had burrowed into, he soon had the fish lying on the grassy bank. He reckoned it would go nearly three pounds, a fine specimen by any standards, as bright as a coin.

After only a moment's hesitation, Powell dispatched the trout and placed it in his fishing bag. The decision whether or not to kill a fish was always a difficult one for him. He generally practiced catch-and-release, which is to say he let most of the fish he caught go, keeping only the occasional one for the table. But this did present an ethical dilemma. Although he had no time for the animal welfare radicals who campaigned to ban fishing on the grounds of cruelty, he was somewhat receptive to the argument that it was more ethical to catch a fish, kill it, and eat it than to catch it simply for the pleasure of playing with it. Unfortunately, there were no longer enough fish to go around for the growing number of people pursuing them, and in many cases, catch-and-release was the only alternative to prohibiting fishing entirely. Powell was able to rationalize all of this because he felt that at some primal level, arising from mankind's hunting antecedents, fishing was a legitimate, indeed a virtuous, pursuit. The pastime provides an opportunity for millions of harried city-dwellers to get closer to nature. Moreover, it is a fact that anglers as a group tend to promote the cause of conservation. Arguably they do this out of self-interest, but were it not for the ever-present angler looking out for his or her favorite stream, Powell was convinced that the country's environment would be far worse off than it was.

With this uplifting thought in mind, Powell lit a cigarette, picked up his rod and bag and, with a feeling of confidence he hadn't experienced for a long time, set off for Mill House. He failed to notice that dark clouds, like unintended consequences, were brewing over the downs.

CHAPTER 26

Powell spent the next morning watching the rain from his window and planning his day. Then before lunch he wandered about the guesthouse, chatting with the new arrivals and generally getting in the way of his host. He intended to ring Sir Reggie first thing after lunch, followed by a visit to Houghton Manor (Jim Hardy had informed him at breakfast that Mrs. Street had invited him to tea at three o'clock). He also wanted to say good-bye to the Reverend Norris at some point. He needed to pay a last call to PC Bailey to compare notes, although he wasn't overly optimistic about the outcome of his last-minute inquiries; and finally, it occurred to him that he really should go round to see Sir Robert Alderson, out of courtesy if nothing else.

At one o'clock he sequestered himself in his room, placed the call, and waited for the familiar voice at the other end.

"Quick."

"Hello, Reggie."

"Oh, it's you." The pathologist didn't sound exactly thrilled.

Powell decided that it was not the time for small talk. "Did you manage to get in touch with your colleague in Aldermaston?" he asked.

"I said I would, didn't I?" the pathologist snapped, clearly miffed about something.

Powell thought it best to say nothing. He heard a commotion in the background and could visualize Sir Reggie rooting around in the untidy piles of papers on his desk like a pig searching for truffles.

"I had him fax the postmortem report this morning, but I can't seem to find the bloody thing." Then a clatter and a sharp expletive. "Who put that bloody cup there?" More rustling and muttering, followed eventually by a triumphant grunt. There was a lengthy pause as he skimmed through the report. "Now then, Powell, what exactly was it you wanted to know?"

Best to ease into it, Powell thought. "For starters, can you tell me how far along her pregnancy was?"

"About three months, give or take."

Powell did a quick calculation. He frowned. "Around the time Garrett left Houghton Bridge. Give or take."

"Would you mind terribly getting to the point."

"The conventional wisdom is that Maggie Stewart committed suicide. I was wondering if there were any other possibilities."

"The photographs show unmistakable indications of hanging," Sir Reggie responded. "A deep furrow on the neck slanting upward in the classic 'V' configuration toward the point of suspension"—more rustling of paper—"which I believe in this case was the branch of a tree. Furthermore, the impression left on the skin by the noose clearly shows the weave of the rope used. I must tell you, Powell, that virtually *all* hangings are suicidal. Homicidal hangings are extremely rare. It would be virtually impossible for one adult to hang another, even where a considerable difference in physical strength existed. Without leaving other marks of violence on the body, that is."

"Suppose the victim was rendered unconscious first, followed by a staged hanging to make it look like suicide?"

Sir Reggie considered this suggestion for a moment. "It's possible to produce noose marks after death," he admitted, "provided that the body is hanged within two hours or so. But again, one would normally expect to see signs of trauma associated with the actual cause of death."

"And there was no indication of anything like that in Maggie Stewart's case?"

"Nothing that jumps out." The pathologist seemed about to add something, but checked himself.

Powell had a flash of inspiration. "What about strangulation?"

"I assume you mean strangulation by some means other than hanging?"

"Right."

There was a short pause. "I'm impressed, Powell. That's a very intriguing thought and, in light of your rather curious preoccupation with what appears to be a straightforward case, I considered the possibility myself." Sir Reggie made this observation offhandedly, much as one might announce the value of some routine scientific measurement. Nonetheless, Powell took it as a compliment.

"But first," the pathologist continued, shifting into lecture mode, "you need to understand the basics. Strangulation is a form of asphyxia in which the cause of death is cerebral hypoxia resulting from compression or occlusion of the vessels supplying blood to the brain. The mechanism is basically the same whether the victim is hanged or strangled, either manually or with a ligature. Dealing first with hanging, contrary to popular opinion, compression of the airway is not necessary to cause death. As a matter of fact," Sir Reggie added, getting into the swing of things, "there are a number of cases where individuals have hanged themselves with a noose placed above the larynx and a permanent tracheostomy opening below."

"Fascinating," Powell observed dryly.

"Along the same lines," Sir Reggie went on, "fractures of the neck are not normally observed in nonjudicial hangings. It basically comes down to obstructing the carotid or vertebral arteries and shutting off the flow of oxygenated blood to the brain. As far as other possible causes of strangulation go, I think we can rule out the use of a ligature in this case—a garrote or something of the sort."

"How so?"

"If a ligature is used, the mark or furrow tends to

encircle the neck in a more or less horizontal plane, depending on the relative heights of the assailant and victim. The chance of such a mark lining up exactly with a subsequent noose mark would be remote. Which leaves us," Sir Reggie concluded, "with the possibility of manual strangulation where the assailant uses his hands or arm to strangle his victim. Normally, there are a number of forensic indications that distinguish manual strangulation from hanging, but it can get a bit complicated."

Powell sighed. "When is it ever *not* complicated?"

The pathologist ignored him. "In most cases of manual strangulation there are petechiae of the conjunctivae, which are generally absent in hangings—"

Throwing caution to the wind, Powell felt compelled to interrupt. "Petechiae of the what?"

"Rupture of the blood vessels in the head due to increased intravascular pressure and congestion. As I explained earlier," Sir Reggie continued, showing an uncharacteristic degree of patience, "death by strangulation results from compression of the blood vessels in the neck. The amount of pressure required to occlude the carotid arteries at the front of the neck is eleven pounds; for the vertebral arteries at the back it is sixty-six pounds; and for the jugular veins it is only four point four pounds. In manual strangulation the pressure is often not sufficient to fully close off all of the blood vessels in the neck. Blood continues to flow into the head by way of the vertebral arteries but cannot escape through the compressed jugular veins. And the assailant may have to alter his grip several times as the victim struggles, resulting in intermittent compression. Waves of blood rush in and out of the head, causing blood pressure to surge and vessels to rupture."

"Lovely," Powell remarked.

"In hangings, by way of contrast, there is generally a complete blockage of the arteries, so there is no accumulation of blood in the head, no increase in pressure, and therefore no hemorrhaging."

"What about Maggie Stewart's case?"

"Interestingly, there was a moderate degree of hemorrhaging typical of manual strangulation and atypical of hanging. I should add however that petechiae do occur in about twenty-five percent of hangings."

"Did the pathologist who conducted the postmortem comment on this?"

"The findings didn't *preclude* hanging, and everything else seemed to point in that direction."

"Such as?" Powell inquired.

"How about an unwanted pregnancy?"

"There was no suicide note," Powell pointed out.

"Unusual, but hardly unprecedented. Desperate people often do things on the spur of the moment."

"Were there any other marks on the neck?" Powell persisted. "I would assume that the finger marks one sees in manual strangulation would be absent in a hanging."

"Not necessarily. In most cases of manual strangulation one *does* see abrasions, contusions, fingernail marks on the skin, that sort of thing—and to answer your question, there were in fact some signs of this in Maggie Stewart's case."

Powell tried unsuccessfully to interrupt.

"There can also be fractures of the hyoid bone or thyroid cartilage," Sir Reggie continued, "although this is more common in older individuals. However, a careful dissection of the neck would be required to determine this, which wasn't done in this case."

"Why am I not surprised?" Powell rejoined.

"See here, Powell, there was no reason at the time to suspect anything other than suicide. In retrospect, the pathologist could have delved a little more deeply into the matter, but we all have more than enough to do and not enough hours in the day to do it. You of all people should know that. If the powers that be would give us the bloody resources we need, we would all do a better job. And just to be clear, Powell, this isn't a matter of the medical profession closing ranks to suppress some instance of gross incompetence. It's just that these things aren't black and white."

Powell sighed. "All right, Reggie, you've convinced me. But how do you explain the finger marks on Maggie Stewart's neck?"

"It's not that unusual. Marks of this nature can be caused by the victim's own struggles to loosen the noose."

"Good God! You mean they sometimes change their minds?"

"It's a macabre thought, isn't it, but then death by hanging can't be a pleasant experience. In any case, one *should* be able to tell the difference between self-inflicted injuries of this type and the characteristic finger imprints seen in most cases of manual strangulation. Give me a minute and I'll have another look at the photographs."

Powell tried to empty his mind as he waited for Sir Reggie's pronouncement. He found the rhythmic rasp of the pathologist's breath on the other end of the line strangely soothing, like a mantra. He thought about Marion, about the soft sound of her breathing as she lay beside him in bed, how it was the last thing he'd hear after making love when he would have been content never to wake up. The pathologist's voice jolted him from his meditation.

"I can't be one hundred percent certain, but it *is* conceivable . . ." He trailed off thoughtfully.

Powell's mental antennae began to vibrate. "Reggie, what are you saying?"

The pathologist took a deep breath. "I think you might be onto something."

CHAPTER 27

The Reverend Geoffrey Norris picked up the telephone. His hand was trembling. "St. Andrew's vicarage."

Powell frowned. The voice on the other end was barely audible.

"Geoffrey, it's Erskine. Is everything all right?"

"Y-yes, yes, of course." The vicar paused to listen. He looked with concern at the woman sitting beside him, her bruised cheek and frightened eyes, wondering about the kind of man who would strike a defenseless woman and the kind of world where such things were commonplace. "Four-thirty? Yes, that would be fine. N-no, no of course not, I look forward to it." There was a lengthy silence. The vicar's face turned pale, like claret draining from a glass. He swallowed with some difficulty. "I see." His voice was flat, devoid of emotion. "Erskine, I m-must go—I have a parishioner with me. Yes, yes—until then. Good-bye." He replaced the receiver in its cradle, reluctant to meet his companion's eyes.

"What is it?" she asked, fearing the worst.

He looked up. "That was the p-policeman I was telling you about." He hesitated. "I don't quite know how to t-tell you this, but he's been looking into Maggie Stewart's death, and it appears—" he drew a deep breath "—it appears that it wasn't suicide after all. He thinks that she may have been m-murdered."

As Powell walked up the lane, the impressive facade of Houghton Manor looming ahead, he made a mental list of the questions he wanted to ask Pamela Street. He knew that he would need to be extremely careful. He also knew that he could be dead wrong, but his instincts told him otherwise. He would have been the first to admit that the foundation upon which he had constructed his house of conjecture was entirely circumstantial; still, everything seemed to point in the same direction.

A popular local girl, Maggie Stewart, falls in love with Richard Garrett, the son of a prominent London solicitor. But it seems that Garrett, Sr., a member of the exclusive Mayfly Fishing Club around which village life in Houghton Bridge revolves, had other plans for his son's future. Maggie, for reasons that are not entirely clear, ends the relationship, although it is widely believed amongst the villagers—including her brother, Brian, her best friend, Danica Hughes, and her uncle, the proprietor of the Coach and Horses—that she was jilted by her lover. A few months later, alone and pregnant—by somebody other than Richard Garrett—she apparently takes her own life.

Except it wasn't suicide. Someone had seized her by

the neck and squeezed the life out of her. No doubt she would have fought back, clawing desperately with her fingers, kicking frantically. She was young and fit, but if her assailant had grabbed her from behind, wearing gloves perhaps to protect his hands, his groin and eyes out of reach, she wouldn't have stood a chance. After ten seconds or so her struggles would have subsided as her brain, deprived of oxygen, began to shut down. But he would likely have continued to press his fingers into her for another minute or so to make sure the job was finished. Then, when she was finally still, he had tightened a noose around her neck and strung her up from a tree beside the Houghton Brook. Powell could visualize the body twisting slowly at the end of the rope. It had been a cold, callous, and cowardly act, and for the first time Powell admitted to himself that he would not be able to let this one go, not until it was finished.

When the door of Houghton Manor opened, Powell did not expect to see Simon Street. The actor's eyes swept over him. "What do you want?" he growled.

"My name's Powell. I'm here to see Mrs. Street."

A glimmer of recognition in his expression. "Oh, yes, you're the chap from Mill House—the historian. I'm afraid Pamela had to pop out. I have no idea when she'll be back."

"I'll call back later then."

A steely smile. "Perhaps I can help, to save you the trouble."

"That's very kind of you."

The actor swung the door wide open. "I'm Simon

Street," he announced grandly, as if expecting Powell to request an autograph. When there was no response, he frowned. "You look familiar. Do I know you from somewhere?"

Powell smiled, remembering their brief encounter in the Coach and Horses and later on the Houghton Brook. "No, I don't think so."

Street shrugged. "We can talk in my study."

The grand entrance hall with its high ornate ceiling gave way to a long corridor, along which Powell followed the lord of the Manor. The scuffed green walls and faded carpet illuminated by a row of pallid yellow lights conveyed the impression that the place had seen better days. There was a vague musty smell, and he heard the sound of a distant door slamming. A domestic scurrying for cover? he wondered.

Street ushered him into a smallish room with a massive desk in the center, a few tatty chairs, and a well-stocked drinks cabinet under the window. The paneled walls were cluttered with framed photographs.

Street turned. "Can I offer you a drink?"

"No, thank you."

Street frowned. "Well, *I* could use one." He walked over to the cabinet.

While he was thus occupied, Powell stood examining one of the photographs. A familiar figure in the center with a younger Street hovering on the periphery. He heard Street behind him.

"That's me with Foo Kendall."

"Way in the back, you mean?"

"That's right," Street replied frostily.

"Are you still active on the stage, Mr. Street?"

The actor sighed dramatically. "Unfortunately, one finds it difficult to find the time, given the demands of managing the estate and so on. But it's in the blood, Mr. Powell. One longs to tread the boards once again."

"I see."

Street glanced at his watch. "Pull up a chair and we can get started." He strolled over to the desk and sat down behind it.

When Powell was settled across from him, Street examined him shrewdly. "Now then, what is your interest in Houghton Bridge?"

"I'm seeking information about a young woman named Maggie Stewart. I may include her story in a book I'm writing about tragedy in the English country village. The account will be fictionalized, of course. Did you know her, by any chance?"

"I know *of* her. Everyone in Houghton Bridge knows about Maggie Stewart." He shook his head sadly. "A young person taking her own life like that. Such a waste, don't you think?"

"Yes, it's very sad. I understand that she used to do housekeeping work around the village and I was wondering if she ever worked here at the Manor."

Street furrowed his brow thoughtfully. "No, I don't think so. I'm sure I would remember if she had. However, my wife normally attends to such things. I could ask her if you wish."

"Don't bother; it was just a shot in the dark. But can you tell me anything about Maggie, anything at all?"

Street shrugged. "Only what I've heard. It's a tragedy, all right, there is no question about that. The poor girl had the misfortune to fall in love with a cad who took advantage of her and left her to fend for herself." He looked at Powell. "It seems she had no one to turn to."

"This cad you refer to, I take it you're referring to that young chap—what's his name?—the one who was found dead up at the weir the other day."

Street nodded, his eyes hard. "His name was Richard Garrett."

"That's the one. A real piece of work, was he?"

"Him and the rest of those toffee-nosed bastards in the Mayfly Club. They swan about the village like they own the fucking place!"

Powell was surprised by the vehemence of Street's outburst. "Tell me about the Mayfly Club," he urged. "Everyone I talk to in Houghton Bridge seems to mention it."

Street smiled smoothly, having regained his composure. "You must forgive me, Mr. Powell, but being a man of humble beginnings myself, I find such throwbacks to our feudal past extremely distasteful." There wasn't a hint of irony his voice. "I am doing my own small part," he pronounced, "to drag Houghton Bridge kicking and screaming into the twenty-first century."

Powell evinced a curious air.

"Most outsiders don't know this," Street continued, "but Houghton Manor, not the Mayfly Club, owns all of the fishing on the Houghton Brook. Due to certain commitments made in the past, we let the rights on portions of the stream to the Mayfly Club and Mill House. The club owns their own fishing on the Test, but the Houghton Brook stretch is the Jewel in the Crown, so to speak." He lowered his voice in a conspiratorial manner. "The thing is, if the Manor is ever sold, they lose their rights."

"What would happen to Jim Hardy at Mill House?" Powell inquired casually.

Street seemed slightly surprised by the question but affected a sympathetic smile, which came across as faintly carnivorous. "Don't you worry about old Jim. I'll take care of him."

"Are you planning on selling Houghton Manor, then?"

Street smiled. "Let's just say that there have been several expressions of interest. The demand for chalk stream fishing has soared in recent years."

"Getting back to Richard Garrett," Powell prompted, "it seems rather telling that he was killed near the place where Maggie Stewart committed suicide. Do you think there could possibly be a connection?"

"Your guess is as good as mine. But there is no denying that many people in the village blamed Garrett for what happened to Ms. Stewart."

"Anyone in particular come to mind?"

Street tossed him a sharp glance. "Isn't that sort of question more properly the province of the police?"

Powell smiled. "I'd like my account to be as realistic as possible."

Street did not seem entirely convinced. "Do you have any identification with you?" he asked.

Powell's mind raced. Just like in rugby, he thought grimly, the best defense is a good offense. "Will a business card do?"

"That would be a good start."

Powell extracted a card from his wallet and handed it over. If he had expected a reaction from the actor he would have been disappointed.

Street looked up. His expression was composed and he blinked placidly at Powell. "Now then, Chief Superintendent, don't you think it's about time you told me what this is all about?"

CHAPTER 28

Powell explained that he was assisting the local police in the Garrett matter and was looking into the possibility that the murder might be related to Maggie Stewart's suicide, given their personal relationship. Simply as a matter of routine, you understand. And if Mr. Street was at all concerned he could telephone PC Bailey for confirmation.

Street smiled smoothly. "I don't think that will be necessary, Chief Superintendent. But why didn't you tell me all this in the first place?"

"Just between you and me, Mr. Street, people tend to get a bit nervous when they're confronted by a policeman, so I like to put them at ease."

Street cocked a skeptical eyebrow. "By impersonating a writer?"

Powell smiled. "I suppose I'm just a frustrated actor."

"Ha, ha! Chief Superintendent, that's very good."

"Of course," Powell continued earnestly, "if I actually

suspected someone of committing a crime I'd have to warn them. It wouldn't do to trample on anyone's rights."

"I'm all for the civil liberties myself," Street replied. "For law-abiding citizens, that is." He looked at Powell. "Since you're off-duty, in a manner of speaking, are you sure I can't interest you in a drink? I've got a bottle of the Macallan that I've been saving for a special occasion and, well, you look like the sort of man who would appreciate it."

"Why not, Mr. Street, why not, indeed?"

Powell thought about the risk he was taking. If he managed to get out of this one with his career intact it would be a bloody miracle. On the other hand, if he did get drummed out of the force for abusing his authority, it would certainly simplify his personal life. He wondered about the job prospects for an unemployed policeman in Canada. But as he sipped his whisky, he couldn't deny that corruption had its compensations.

Simon Street leaned back in his chair. "Now then, Chief Superintendent, where were we? Oh, yes, you were asking me who in the village blamed Richard Garrett for Ms. Stewart's suicide. Where to start? There's her uncle, Harry Watts, the proprietor of the Coach and Horses. He's a common sort of fellow and he's always going on about it. Besides that, he has my vote as the most unpleasant publican in Britain, and I've known quite a few in my time. Ha, ha!"

Powell nodded. "I've had the pleasure. Anyone else come to mind?"

Street frowned thoughtfully. "Well there is Ms. Stewart's

friend Danica Hughes. Her father was the former river-keeper for the Mayfly Club. Ms. Hughes and Ms. Stewart were inseparable. But now that I think about it, I believe Ms. Hughes was away having it off with the present river-keeper, John Miller, when Ms. Stewart took her own life."

"You certainly are a gold mine of information, Mr. Street."

An odd expression flashed across Street's face. "Yes, well, I like to take an active interest in village affairs."

"Please continue. I find this most informative."

Street hesitated. "Well, this is a bit awkward—I mean, one doesn't wish to single out the disadvantaged, but one can't avoid mentioning Ms. Stewart's brother, Brian. . . ."

"I hear he's completely loony," Powell volunteered.

"Bloody bonkers. I wouldn't put anything past that one."

"I take it from what you've said that there is no short-age of people in Houghton Bridge happy to see Richard Garrett dead. My next question to you is this: Which of them is capable of cold-blooded murder?"

"I'm not sure I would put it quite so directly, Chief Superintendent, but I can tell you that most people around these parts feel that Garrett got what he deserved for what he did to Ms. Stewart."

"Is that what *you* think, Mr. Street?"

Street smiled equably. "I am a simple actor, Chief Superintendent—I reserve my passion for the stage. As the Bard said: '*Give me a man that is not passion's slave, and I will wear him in my heart's core.*'"

Powell stared at Street as he spoke. "'*Is it not mon-*

strous that this player here, but in a fiction, in a dream of
passion, could force his soul so to his own conceit?'" he
responded.

The actor was clearly unnerved. "I beg your pardon?"

"I couldn't help noticing that throughout our conversation you have referred to Maggie Stewart as 'Ms. Stewart.' "

"What of it?"

"You knew her much better than that, didn't you,
Simon?"

"What are you talking about?"

"I know for a fact that she worked here at the Manor
and I find it difficult to believe you wouldn't remember
her. From what I've heard she was an attractive young
woman, and you do have an eye for ladies, don't you,
Simon?"

Street's face tightened into an expressionless mask.
"She may have worked here—they all look alike to me—
but as I told you before, my wife deals with the domes-
tics. In any case I don't make a habit of shagging the
help."

"Let me tell you what I think happened and then I'll
give you an opportunity to correct me if I'm wrong."

"Will you now?" He hesitated. "Upon reflection, I
think it might be best if you told it to my solicitor." He
reached for the telephone.

"We can do this at the police station if you prefer."

The actor didn't miss a beat. "See here, Chief Superintendent, I wouldn't want you to end up looking foolish in
the eyes of your superiors. I have no idea what you are

trying to get at, but I am prepared to hear you out and set you straight."

"Then I'll begin, shall I? At the time Maggie Stewart broke up with her boyfriend, Richard Garrett, she was working part-time here at the Manor as a housekeeper. I will confirm this with Mrs. Street when I see her. It was Maggie's decision to end the relationship and I believe she was heartbroken—"

"Wait a minute," Street interrupted. "That doesn't make any sense. Why would she have ended it, then?"

"That's a good question, Simon. I think it's because Richard's father did not approve of the relationship."

Street laughed. "Do you honestly think that would have deterred her? Young people these days don't seem to care very much what their parents think."

"True. But I think Maggie was different. From all accounts Richard had a promising legal career ahead of him. Perhaps she worried about fitting into his social circle; maybe she thought she'd hold him back somehow. We'll never know. But I shouldn't need to tell you that the class system is alive and well in this country. Its biggest supporters these days are the nouveau riche and social climbers who aspire to the gentry but aren't interested in the responsibility that goes with it."

Street sneered. "I don't need a lecture from you on noblesse oblige. Garrett was a fucking wanker and she was a slut. They both got what they deserved."

"Your candor is refreshing, Simon, which brings us to the next chapter in our sordid little story. It probably happened soon after Maggie broke up with Garrett. Maggie reported to work at the Manor and your wife was out. Perhaps she was feeling particularly sorry for herself that day. In any case, I'm sure you were at your charming best. Sit here beside me, my dear, and have a drink. Tell old Simon all about it. The point is, you got what you wanted from her and she ended up pregnant."

Street laughed uproariously. "You can't be serious! I can do much better than the likes of Maggie Stewart any day of the week. Besides, everybody knows that Richard Garrett put her in the pudding club."

Powell ignored him. "Maggie wanted to keep her baby, so she came to you for financial assistance. She probably planned to go away and start a new life. Perhaps she threatened to expose you if you didn't help her. But you couldn't have your wife finding out about your dalliance with the housemaid, could you, Simon? You hadn't been married that long and I would hazard a guess that you didn't wield quite the same degree of influence over your wife back then as you do now. When you can threaten her with financial ruin every time she doesn't do what you want."

Street smiled icily. "I wouldn't abandon that writing career just yet, Chief Superintendent. This will make a great piece of fiction."

Powell forged ahead. "You arranged to meet her at the weir one evening to talk it over. It's secluded enough there that you weren't likely to be observed by anyone. At some point, when she turned away from you, you saw your chance. You had it all planned out, didn't you, Simon? After you'd strangled her, you used the rope you'd brought with you to hang her body from the nearest tree to make it look like suicide. You were very clever, Simon, but not clever enough. You should have quit while you were ahead."

Street stared at him in amazement. "I have no idea what you're talking about."

"I think you do."

Street smiled with a chilling absence of emotion. "Your whole case hinges on the supposition that I impregnated the young lady. I deny it, of course, but either way you'll never be able to prove it."

"Have you ever heard of deoxyribonucleic acid, Simon?"

"What?"

"DNA. You obviously haven't kept up with the advances in forensic science."

Street swallowed but said nothing.

"Tissue samples from postmortems are routinely retained in a sort of archive," Powell lied, "just in case they're ever needed. In this case, the fetus was preserved. If foul play were ever suspected in Maggie Stewart's death, it would be a simple matter to do a genetic comparison with a strand of hair taken from the suspect or a swab from the inside of his cheek. The test is virtually foolproof."

Street thought about this for a moment. "But you'd need grounds to obtain a warrant for your sample, wouldn't you?" he said. "And even if I were the father, it wouldn't prove I killed her, would it? And what about Richard Garrett?" he continued with increasing confi-

dence in his voice. "You implied some connection between his murder and what happened to Maggie. What
could I possibly have to gain by killing him?"

"First off, I have to say that leaving him pinned in the
sluice gate like that was a bit, er, theatrical. But to answer
your question, I think he found out about you and Maggie
and threatened to expose you. You couldn't allow that to
happen, could you, Simon? Even now I suspect there are
limits to Mrs. Street's tolerance."

Street turned a deathly pale. Then suddenly, hope for
an Oscar nomination fading fast, he sprang from his
chair, his voice swelling to a crescendo of indignant fury.
"This is an outrage!" he roared. "I won't stand for it another minute! I'll have you know that Pamela knows the
chief constable personally, and I have no doubt he will be
very interested in the scandalous manner in which you
have conducted yourself. Impersonating a civilian, abusing my hospitality, and then confronting me—a pillar of
the community—with these absurd allegations. Now get
out, I tell you! Get out!"

CHAPTER 29

On his way to St. Andrew's, Powell stopped by the Mayfly Inn with the best of intentions. He didn't remember ordering his drink, just sitting at his table nursing his frustration. He knew he was right about Street, but he also knew he'd never be able to prove it in a court of law. And he had little doubt that Street was onto him, secure in the knowledge that his whole bloody case was founded on unsubstantiated conjecture. Simon Street wasn't much of an actor, but he wasn't stupid either. Powell polished off his pint and got up for another.

It was bad enough that a cold-blooded murderer was getting off scot-free—it wouldn't be the first time, after all—but by sticking his nose where it didn't belong he had probably sabotaged what was left of his career in the process. If Street ever placed that call to the local chief constable, he might as well pack his bags and board the next plane to Canada. Not wanting to travel any farther down that particular road, Powell tried to stay focused on the problem at hand.

He was certain about Maggie Stewart; Richard Garrett's murder was more problematic. It all came down to motive. As Street himself had rhetorically put it: What would he have to gain by killing Garrett? If in fact Garrett knew about Maggie and Street, how did he find out? It was unlikely that Maggie would have told him. More likely he discovered the truth after coming back to Houghton Bridge. One possibility was a chance encounter on the stream with Street. It was common knowledge that there was no love lost between them. Garrett knew that Street had poached a fish on the club water and Street had been going off at the mouth recently about selling the estate and with it the rights to the Mayfly Club's fishing. Words were likely exchanged and one thing led to another. Powell wouldn't put it past Street to drag Maggie's name into it. Perhaps he had bragged about his conquest, rubbed Garrett's face in it. He probably thought—if he thought about it at all—that Garrett would keep it to himself, to protect the reputation of his dead lover.

But in a perverse way, the revelation would likely have been liberating for Garrett. Here was the key to the puzzle that had haunted him for so many years, the explanation for Maggie's suicide. The feelings of guilt and self-recrimination could finally be exorcized. Anger and hurt would quickly give way to the desire for revenge. And what better way to get back at Street than to threaten to tell his wife. Everyone knew that Street was a gigolo and that Mrs. Street, whatever human frailties she possessed, was an honorable woman who could be relied on to do the right thing. Unfortunately, Richard Garrett made a huge mistake when he crossed Simon Street and he got his head caved in for his trouble.

Powell stared into the dregs of his beer for inspiration. He had to admit that it was all speculation and he had taken it about as far as he could. He drained his glass and thought about having another. Why not, he thought, beginning to feel thoroughly sorry for himself. He decided that it might be best to ring the vicar and postpone his visit until tomorrow morning. As it turned out there was no answer at St. Andrew's, so Powell left a message on the vicar's answerphone. It would turn out to be a decision he would live to regret.

Powell remembered little of the night before, but from the way his head felt, he reckoned it was just as well. When he came down to breakfast there was an urgent message from PC Bailey awaiting him. Jim Hardy directed him to the phone in the office.

"Yes, Bailey, what is it?"

"It's Simon Street, sir. He seems to have disappeared."

"What?"

"Missing, sir, vanished without a trace."

Powell felt a surge of energy. It looked like the rat had bolted. "You mean he's left the village for parts unknown?"

"Not exactly, sir. From what we can get out of Mrs.

Street, he went out for a walk last evening and didn't come back. Left his car and wallet at the Manor. We suspect foul play."

Powell felt exhilaration quickly give way to confusion and self-doubt. How could he have been so far off the mark? Had he been so preoccupied with Simon Street, like a trout focused on a fisherman's fly, that he had been oblivious to the bigger picture? Was Street now the third victim of a cold-blooded murderer who was still at large? Someone he had previously discounted, or perhaps not even considered at all? His head was awhirl with the possibilities, and he found it difficult to think clearly. "Give me a few minutes, Bailey, and I'll come down to the station."

"Yes, sir."

"More coffee," Powell grunted, shoving his cup over to PC Bailey, who was presiding at the urn. "When did you say Mrs. Street reported Street missing?"

"This morning, sir. Around eight-thirty."

"I thought you said he went out last night."

"That's what Mrs. Street said, sir."

"Then why did she wait until eight-thirty this morning to report it?"

"Apparently she went to bed early last night and only discovered that Mr. Street hadn't come home when she got up this morning."

"Does she have any idea where he might have gone?"

"No, sir. Apparently she wasn't at home when he went out."

Powell frowned. "Then how did she know that he'd gone out for a walk?"

PC Bailey shrugged. "She was in quite a state when I talked to her, and to tell you the truth, sir, I don't think she knew whether she was coming or going."

"Upset, was she?"

"Sounded like it. I passed her on to Sergeant Potter straightaway, but I thought you should know about it, sir."

Powell lapsed into a lengthy silence, his mind wandering. He thought about his visit to Houghton Manor yesterday afternoon. It occurred to him for the first time that Pamela Street's absence was very odd after having invited him to tea. From what he knew of her it was entirely out of character. Then he suddenly remembered he still had to pay a visit to St. Andrew's. He looked at PC Bailey, wondering how much he should reveal of his suspicions about Simon Street, given the latest turn of events. Something was nagging away at the back of his mind but he couldn't put his finger on it. He recalled the actor quoting Hamlet.

"I think, Bailey," he said wearily, "something is rotten in the County of Hampshire."

Then it struck him with the numbing shock of certainty. He felt sick to his stomach as the enormity of the realization sunk in.

"' *'Tis an unweeded garden that grows to seed; things rank and gross in nature possess it merely. That it should come to this!* '"

"Sir?"

Powell explained as quickly as he could, leaving the

young constable incredulous. "God Almighty! W-what should we do, sir?" he stammered.

Powell trudged up the long hill to St. Andrew's, his mind as empty as the ambiguous gray sky. He felt clammy and slightly out of breath. He thought about a cigarette, as he always did at a time like this, but managed to resist the urge. The door to the church was open, so he stepped into the gloom and called out. There was no answer. He walked over to the vicarage and knocked, but no one came to the door. In the churchyard he stood still and listened. He could hear the faint *clink* of metal on stone somewhere round the back.

He found the Reverend Geoffrey Norris in the graveyard. The vicar looked up from his digging and raised his arm in greeting. His large face was flushed and traced with rivulets of sweat. "I've been expecting you," he said breathlessly. "Would you care for some tea?"

"Yes, Geoffrey, that would be nice."

"You know, don't you?"

Powell nodded.

"We should have rung the police immediately, of course, but I knew you were coming this morning. . . ." He trailed off. "Forgive me; I must look a fright. I've been up half the night but I'm nearly finished now. I wanted to do the right thing by him, you understand."

"I understand."

The vicar's expression was strangely placid, and Powell noticed that he wasn't stuttering anymore.

"You mustn't blame yourself, Erskine, there is nothing you could have done. It wasn't something I planned—it was an accident, really—but I couldn't bear to see him treat Pamela like that." He sighed gently. "But what's done is done and I am content to face my Maker." His eyes welled with tears. "The thing is, Erskine, I wouldn't want you to think any less of me. I mean, I couldn't bear it if you—"

Powell placed his hand on the vicar's shoulder. "Why don't we talk about it over a cup of tea?"

EPILOGUE

Back in Surbiton, Powell found himself at loose ends. Far from feeling pleased with himself, and faced with the prospect of returning to work on Monday morning, not to mention the call to Marion he had been putting off since he had arrived home, he elected to sit and stare out the window, attempting to sort out his feelings. It wasn't much of an existence, he thought as he lit a cigarette, swinging like a pendulum from one emotional extreme to the other. The only time he felt really happy, really alive, was when he was immersed in a case. He used to think he was manic-depressive, or something bordering on it. A bipolar bull in an existential china shop.

Then he had come to the conclusion that he had a tendency toward depression, which made him feel even more inadequate, even though he knew it was just a biochemical defect, like having an allergy to something. He wondered half-seriously if one could be allergic to the routine of everyday life. Anyway, it was nothing that two fingers of the Macallan couldn't put right, at least for an hour or two. He reached for the bottle.

As he looked out over his back garden, or what was left of it, he couldn't help thinking about the Reverend Geoffrey Norris, tending his congregation like a garden of bright and beautiful flowers in the village of Houghton Bridge. Powell wondered, with more than a twinge of remorse, what was going to become of the vicar. If he hadn't stopped off at the pub on the way to St. Andrew's that afternoon, it might have turned out differently. But, as the vicar himself had put it, what's done is done.

Powell had suspected all along that the vicar knew who the father of Maggie Stewart's baby was, and after he had let it slip that the girl's death had been something other than a suicide, he had begun to worry that the clergyman might put two and two together. But as it turned out, the vicar had been preoccupied not with Maggie's murder, but instead with Pamela Street's welfare. It seemed that Simon Street, increasingly frustrated by Pamela's refusal to comply with his wishes, had resorted to physically abusing her. Reluctant to sully the family reputation by reporting her husband to the police, Pamela had come to rely on frequent visits to St. Andrew's for comfort and sympathy from the vicar, which is where she had gone on the afternoon Powell paid a visit to Houghton Manor.

After Powell had left the Manor, Street had driven in a rage to St. Andrew's to collect his wife. When she had refused to go with him, he had attempted to drag her off. The vicar had implored him to stop, but to no effect. In desperation, he had grabbed the nearest weapon to hand—a fire poker—and struck Street once on the back. As Street had turned to deal with the vicar, he slipped and hit his head on the corner of the coffee table. He was dead in minutes.

Severely shaken by what had happened, and in an unfortunate lapse of judgment, Mrs. Street and the vicar concocted a hasty story to explain Street's disappearance—the one she related to the police the following morning. Mrs. Street had driven back to the Manor in Street's car, leaving the vicar to bury the body.

Powell had no reason to doubt that it had happened exactly as the Reverend Geoffrey Norris had recounted it. Simon Street, it had to be said, got no more than he deserved, and Powell was fairly certain that a court of law would see it the same way. With any luck, he thought, the vicar would not miss a Sunday service at St. Andrew's.

He stabbed out his cigarette, the bitter taste of nicotine in his throat. It really was a filthy habit. He sat motionless for several minutes thinking about what he was about to do. Life was all about taking little steps, he knew, each one insignificant in itself but irreversible in their totality. He took a deep breath and reached for the telephone. He punched in the numbers on the crumpled scrap of paper and waited for what seemed like ages. Eventually someone picked up, and he heard a voice asking him what he needed. He hesitated for only a second.

"Jemma Walker," he said.

If you enjoyed *Malice Downstream*, don't miss
Erskine Powell's earlier adventures. . .

MALICE IN
THE HIGHLANDS
The first Erskine Powell mystery

by Graham Thomas

Crime, investigation, punishment. They're all in a
day's work to Detective-Chief Superintendent
Erskine Powell of New Scotland Yard. Seeking
distance from criminal concerns, Powell embarks
on a salmon-fishing competition in the Scottish
Highlands. But there, in the castle-dotted
countryside along the picturesque River Spey, a
cold-blooded murderer soon turns Powell's haven
into a busman's holiday—and a quiet anglers'
paradise becomes just as deadly as the mean
streets of London. . . .

Published by Fawcett Books.
Available wherever books are sold.

MALICE IN CORNWALL

by Graham Thomas

On the north coast of Cornwall, residents in the quaint seaside town of Penrick report a terrifying phenomenon—an eerie, glowing apparition that rides the surf at night. Yet Chief Superintendent Powell soon learns that Penrick already harbors unsolved mysteries. For, thirty years ago, someone killed a teenager and left her body to wash up on Penrick Sands—precisely where the apparition now appears. In fact, Powell faces not one but two strangely intertwined puzzles and a double-edged sword of menace. . . .

Published by Fawcett Books.
Available wherever books are sold.

MALICE ON THE MOORS

by Graham Thomas

On a remote estate in the North York Moors, a murderer lays a cunning trap. The prey, it seems, is Dickie Dinsdale, the greedy landowner who bulldozes people's lives like so many old barns. Easily a dozen residents of Blackamoor would derive pleasure from Dinsdale's slow, painful death. Suspects are as thick as grouse in summer, and bringing down a killer on the wing is very tricky—even for a pro like Chief Superintendent Erskine Powell. . . .

Published by Fawcett Books.
Available wherever books are sold.

MALICE IN LONDON

by Graham Thomas

When a murder victim is discovered in the murky waters of the River Thames, Erskine Powell of Scotland Yard plunges into the most diabolical case of his distinguished career. A second brutal slaying draws Powell even deeper into a tangled web of greed, deception, and blackmail. From Tower Bridge to Soho, from Mayfair to Bloomsbury, Powell throws a dragnet across London, racing against time to link two savage crimes—and stop a cold-blooded killer dead in his tracks. . . .

Published by Fawcett Books.
Available wherever books are sold.

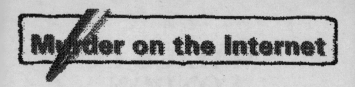

Murder on the Internet

Subscribe to the
MURDER ON THE INTERNET
e-newsletter—and receive all these
fabulous online features directly in
your e-mail inbox:

☠ Previews of upcoming books
☠ In-depth interviews with mystery authors
and publishing insiders
☠ Calendars of signings and readings for
Ballantine mystery authors
☠ Profiles of mystery authors
☠ Mystery quizzes and contests

Two easy ways to subscribe:
Go to www.ballantinebooks.com/mystery
or send a blank e-mail to
join-mystery@list.randomhouse.com.

Murder on the Internet—
the mystery e-newsletter brought to you
by Ballantine Books